Caffeine

Ve

Nick Oldham

Based on a screenplay by

Stephen Reynolds

Published by Caffeine Nights Publishing 2013

Published in Great Britain by Caffeine Nights Publishing

www.caffeine-nights.com

British Library Cataloguing in Publication Data.

A CIP catalogue record for this book is available from the British
Library

INTRODUCTION

As a teenage film enthusiast I used to prowl the second-hand book stores in Brighton for movie tie-in paperbacks. Sometimes, it was a popular novel with a simple sticker on the front. Other times, a more lavish affair with movie stills in the middle. They uniquely combined two of my favourite pastimes – movies and reading. I still have some 200 of them in my house. Sadly, the art of the film tie-in paperback seems to have been lost over the past twenty years or so – perhaps because the internet gives away so much advance information that background on the film is not regarded as such an important part of a film's marketing. Perhaps because distribution became a more scientific, conveyor belt process. Whatever the reason, the fact remains that it is a shame.

When writer/director Stephen Reynolds and I first started discussing the vigilante idea that ultimately became Vendetta, I had no idea it would become such an eagerly-anticipated movie. Steve and I shared a passion for 80s and 90s action movies – Who Dares Wins, Predator, Out For Justice, the Death Wish movies et al – and these soon became our reference points. Initially conceived as a micro-budget vehicle for actor Nick Nevern (after our success with The Rise & Fall of a White Collar Hooligan), Vendetta's stars really aligned when a film Nick was attached to direct was greenlit, making him unavailable, and a call from my old friend Danny Dyer alerted me to the fact that he was looking for a project that got him back to what he does best – a gritty, urban action movie.

It is fair to say that Stephen then turned out one of the most commercial screenplays I have ever read – I knew he could write, but the expertly drawn characters populating a desolate, terrifying metropolis were something else. And the torture scenes… wow – this stuff was dark beyond belief. Needless to say, Danny loved it, and the cast started to fill up with really talented actors – Vincent Regan, Al Petrie, Ricci Harnett, Emma Samms, Roxanne McKee… without a doubt the strongest ensemble cast I have ever put together. As to the finished film – well, judge for yourself. I'm intensely proud of it and genuinely believe that it really delivers everything you'd hope for.

And as to how the book you now hold came about... well those stars aligned once more. I had been sent a book called The Last Big Job by celebrated crime author Nick Oldham. I loved his style of writing and we arranged to meet for a spot of lunch. The idea of a Vendetta novelisation was born at that lunch. I can't think of anyone better than Nick Oldham to expand on the world of Vendetta which Stephen Reynolds so skilfully created. Nick's writing draws you right in and his characters are living, breathing people. A few hours later, I met dashing publisher Darren Laws of Caffeine Nights to talk about him reprinting Dougie Brimson's cult novel Top Dog to tie in with our film adaptation in 2014. Would a Vendetta novelisation be of interest? Yes, it would. And so a partnership was formed between Caffeine Nights and my company, Richwater Films. The first fruit of that partnership is what you hold in your hands now and I hope that it will be the first of many... and who knows, maybe there'll even be another outing for our man James Vickers....

Jonathan Sothcott, Vendetta Film Producer
CEO Richwater Films

'To Belinda, who kept me on track'

Nick Oldham

RICHWATER FILMS presents
a JONATHAN SOTHCOTT production
a STEPHEN REYNOLDS film

DANNY DYER in

VENDETTA

JOSEF ALTIN ROXANNE MCKEE ALISTAIR PETRIE
NICK NEVERN BRUCE PAYNE EMMA SAMMS
TONY DENHAM TAMARYN PAYNE SIMONA BRHLIKOVA
with

RICCI HARNETT and VINCENT REGAN

Make Up Designer FRANCES HOUNSOM Costume Designer
LENKA PADYSAKOVA
Production Designer ANTHONY NEALE Casting Director LEE
MOUNTJOY
Director of Photography HAIDER ZAFAR
Music composed by PHIL MOUNTFORD
Executive Producers RAFAEL QUINTIAN, SIMON CLUETT, WAYNE
HODGSON,
WILL HORN, SIMON MARGOLIS, MARK WATSON-GANDY and
NICK ALDRICH

Produced by JONATHAN SOTHCOTT

Written & Directed by STEPHEN REYNOLDS

PROLOGUE

CAMP BASTION, AFGHANISTAN.

Jimmy Vickers checked and loaded his Sig Sauer P226 pistol, then slid it into the holster on his right hip. He picked up his mug of steaming hot tea and walked across to the door of his office, yawning, rolling his shoulders.

He was ready for home. Just a few more days and he and his gear would be climbing aboard the C17 Transporter plane and once the always hair-raising take off had been accomplished, he would settle himself down, let his body become simpatico with the powerful drum of the aircraft engines and he would probably have the deepest, longest sleep he'd managed in the past six months. When he awoke he would be back in England. Home.

However, there was still work to be done out here. Another few days to go, and this was the first of them as he stood at 3.05am, rubbing his face, lounging by the door at the top of the short flight of wooden steps of his raised, prefabricated office, once again taking in the hum of life that was Camp Bastion. A city on its own, built by Royal Engineers from nothing in the unforgiving terrain of Afghanistan in Helmand Province. It now operated twenty four hours a day, seven days a week, without fail, and had been doing so for over six years.

Jimmy sipped his tea. It was strong and sweet and tasted amazing, probably the most appreciated drink consumed by the British Army. A pint or two of lager at the finish of a long, dusty op was good, necessary, but tea was the mainstay, a complex make up of chemicals that had a calming yet revitalising effect on the human body.

Ask any mum. As he took another sip, Jimmy thought of his own doting mother. He was eager to see her again and be overwhelmed by her chatter that was like being fired at by a Gatling gun, but which Jimmy loved and could endure for hours. Like most soldiers out here, what kept him going was the knowledge that back home there was something solid, people back there who cared and thought of him every hour.

And he was eagerly anticipating a pint with his dad down at The Wolf.

Then, of course, there was Morgan ... Jimmy frowned, sipped some more of his tea and looked across the glowing cupola of unnatural light in the desert that was Bastion, his home for many months. Once again, he found himself in awe of the 'can-do' attitude of the British Army which, in spite of facing constant cutbacks, staff reductions and, obviously, the enemy, still 'did'.

Built in 2006, Bastion was four miles long, two miles wide, in a remote desert area northwest of Lashkar Gah, which was the capital of Helmand Province. Helmand, a name now well known by viewers of the TV news in the UK as an area where, tragically, too many young soldiers had died while serving their country in what appeared to be a fruitless, unwinnable war against the Taliban.

Jimmy Vickers could quote every known fact about Bastion, including that it was supposed to be the safest place in Afghanistan – but that had been proved woefully wrong in September 2012, when the camp was attacked by fifteen Taliban fighters, dressed in US Army uniforms, when two US marines were killed and some aircraft were destroyed. The Taliban had also admitted that one of their targets had been Prince Harry, who was serving in Afghanistan at the time.

Jimmy had been involved in a brutal four hour firefight with the attackers, during which fourteen of the insurgents were killed and a fifteenth injured and captured.

After two days of intensive interrogation by Jimmy, the prisoner revealed that a further attack on Bastion was already underway. A combined strike force of British and US Special Forces ambushed a group of Taliban fighters near Lashkar Gah and slotted every one of them, leaving twenty dead, their blood seeping into the sand.

That had been one of Jimmy's finest moments – and his Colonel, a gruff bear of a man named Leach, cynically passed on thanks from the highest level of the UK government for his work in 'extracting' the information from the injured man that had ultimately saved many lives of the coalition forces. The memory of his right forefinger probing into the man's gunshot wound in his bicep, just above his right elbow, searching out sheared nerve endings, squeezing them hard and hearing the man's blood-curdling screams for mercy would linger with Jimmy for many a year.

Since then, security at Bastion had been re-thought and re-worked. But Jimmy knew that no fortress was impregnable, especially against an enemy as dedicated and cunning as the Taliban.

He flicked the dregs of his first brew of the day onto the gritty ground and stepped back into his office, where the temperature reading inside was a bearable twenty-two degrees. Later that day it would soar to forty-five. Not the hottest it had ever been, but still fucking hot.

He was due to go out on patrol later that day – airlifted by Chinook helicopter to an area forty miles north-east of Bastion, where Intel was that a village had become an Al-Qaeda hideout. This was Intel that Jimmy had put together from a number of sources, and he wanted to be there on the ground to check its veracity – and be part of the op to flush them out if they were there.

He wasn't due to leave for another two hours. What he wanted to do in the meantime was analyse some further Intel and satellite photographs that had just come in about the area. It was his intention to be a shiny-arsed desk jockey for an hour before prepping himself for the off.

He sat down and unfolded a large-scale map of the area, cross-checking references on his laptop and enlarging the satellite images, his eyes squinting thoughtfully at them.

It all looked pretty sound to Jimmy, who was eager to get moving and get it over with. This was probably his last deployment before home, unless something untoward happened.

He leaned back and laced his fingers behind his head, let the office chair tilt and crossed his ankles on the desk.

'Jeez, so it is feckin' true,' came the coarse Scottish accent of Mickey Burton, one of Jimmy's colleagues in the very specialist department in which he worked. 'You really are a lazy-arsed DJ. Always feckin' suspected it.'

Jimmy turned and gazed sceptically at Burton standing in the office door. Burton had become one of his closest friends over the years. He was a big brute of a man – on the outside. He could be brash and nasty unless he was dealt with correctly and to Jimmy's knowledge, only two people had that skill: Jimmy himself and Colonel Leach. However, underneath that veneer, Burton had a sharp, calculating brain which made him a great gatherer and analyst of information and intelligence – and a cold-blooded interrogator of persons he suspected had killed, or knew of others who had killed or planned to kill, British soldiers.

'It's my dream to have an office like this,' Jimmy said.

'And lo-and-behold, yer fecking dream has come true,' Burton said.

'I kinda really thought up the top of the Pineapple in London, though.'

'Ahhh – doin' what? Ye'd feckin' hate it, Jim me lad.'

'I know, I know … but a guy can dream, ey?'

Burton was kitted out in his full combat gear, desert fatigues. He was joining a squad of Duke of Lancaster Regiment boys due to set out on patrol in about half an hour. Jimmy could hear voices outside as they prepared for a walk which could either be the most boring hot day of their lives, or the worst. Jimmy hoped the former. Boring was good. The DLR lads were to be accompanied by a unit of ten Afghan soldiers who had been training with them and were proving their worth nicely, thank you.

Jimmy had not been involved in vetting the Afghans, but he was aware the reports about this particular unit were positive. They had stepped up to the mark during several clashes with insurgents and done their share of killing. It looked as though they were going to be okay, which to be fair, the majority of them were.

Unless, as Jimmy warned constantly about such soldiers, they were playing the long game.

He remained deeply suspicious of all home-grown troops, but realised the necessity of training them up alongside British and US Army personnel. He tried to keep an open mind and not judge them too harshly, because the good ones, by joining forces with the coalition, put themselves and their families under intense pressure and danger.

It was not unknown for an Afghan soldier to return home on leave to discover his family, even his whole village, had been murdered, the buildings razed to the ground by the Taliban.

Not easy, Jimmy conceded.

That day, Burton was going along with them to see what Intel he could glean from a nearby village that had been a hotbed of Taliban activity recently. The patrol was scheduled for somewhere in the region of six hours in the boiling sun. A tough, dehydrating day – and always the possibility that one or more of them would come back by helicopter in a body bag.

'Seems they've come for me,' Burton said, glancing out of the office, seeing the DLR patrol mustering.

'Hey, remember – look left, 'cos they drive on the right,' Jimmy said. Their little warning ritual meaning 'watch your back'. Burton crossed over to Jimmy, swept his feet off the desk, and they shook hands as Jimmy rocked forward. Burton turned and left the office, bawling as he stepped onto the threshold, 'Now me feckin' little lovelies, your hero is amongst you.'

Jimmy grinned, sat forward.

A moment later he heard the devout shout, 'Allahu Akhbar' – God is great.

And the first shot was fired as the long game culminated that morning.

Jimmy's head spun at the first dull 'thuck' of an SLR rifle being fired. And then the world slowed right down, even though everything was really happening at a million miles per hour.

At the door, Mickey Burton's head exploded. Jimmy was convinced he saw the round enter the top of his friend's head and remove a quarter of his skull cap and the left side of his face. Burton staggered backwards, arms flailing. He crashed and tipped over one of the office chairs.

Jimmy dropped behind his desk as four rounds smashed through the thin prefab walls. He rolled across the floor, drawing his Sig as he went, coming up onto one knee by Burton's body. Incredibly, Jimmy saw that Mickey's chest was still rising and falling.

More gunfire. More shouts of alarm.

Jimmy forward-rolled to the office door, bobbed his head out and saw mayhem, but his quick eyes and brain read everything instantly.

Five Taliban infiltrators, masquerading as loyal soldiers of the Afghan army who had successfully ingratiated themselves deep to lull the British into a false sense of security, were unloading their weapons into the unsuspecting DLR lads and members of the Afghan Army. Three Brits fell as Jimmy watched, others dived for cover, returning fire. Screams, shouts, running, bodies everywhere, weapons being discharged. Chaos.

Jimmy swore.

One of the Taliban fell, clutching his chest.

Another dropped to one knee, bringing up his rifle and beading on the back of a running DLR soldier.

Jimmy shot him before he fired, catching him just below his ear, effectively removing the back of his neck. He fell, and the Brit soldier dived into cover, unhurt.

Another Taliban swung towards Jimmy, a machine pistol in his hands, firing as he rotated, smashing holes into the wall of the office building. Jimmy leapt out of the door, launched himself off the top step, hit the ground and rolled, firing as he went, catching him in the right shoulder, spinning him back as the joint exploded sickeningly.

Jimmy came up on both knees.

Other soldiers were pouring onto the scene, trying to make sense of it.

But the two remaining Taliban were about to conclude their suicide mission. They stood back to back and ripped their tunics open, revealing the bombs strapped to their waists. Then they turned to face and embrace each other and screamed simultaneously, 'Allahu Akhbar' in what looked like a pre-planned, rehearsed move.

Jimmy saw what was coming.

He yelled a warning, then scrambled for the prefab and threw himself underneath it as the bombs detonated. The blast was deafening and the force of it flung Jimmy along the ground. His hearing went, his vision blurred and the force of it felt like ten people had kicked him in the side, at the same time as hurling buckets of pebble-dashing over him.

But he was alive and although his head swam and felt like he was holding it in a fish tank, he didn't allow himself to linger and recover. He was a soldier – and knew he had to move. He dragged himself from under the cabin, unsteady on his feet, his brain swirling, but still knowing exactly what had happened. In the rising dust and debris and in a crater made by the blast, he saw that the lower halves of the two Taliban suicide bombers were actually intact. Their upper halves, from the waist up, had been completely obliterated by the explosion. Further away he saw two more bodies and more soldiers running onto the scene.

Jimmy knew then it was all over. Now it was a case of saving lives.

And Mickey Burton had still been breathing despite the horrendous head wound.

He stood swaying, slightly off balance, his ears pounding. He looked at the front of his office and saw that it had been destroyed, the front wall blown away, nothing but matchsticks, dust and papers. He could not see his desk, but he knew that Burton was underneath the debris. He rushed up the steps and began scraping the mess away with his bare hands, digging through until he uncovered the top half of Burton's body now caked in grit and sand.

Jimmy knelt down by his friend.

And God – he was still breathing, although the round had passed through the side of his head and removed a chunk of skull, out of which oozed his brain, a grey-red mushy mess.

'You tough fucker,' Jimmy said, easing his fingers of his right hand under the back of Burton's head. 'Medic!' he yelled. 'Fuckin' medic.' He leaned forwards and gently brushed the dust and grit away from Burton's face with his free hand, aware suddenly of the sensation of holding Burton's brain in the palm of his right hand, warm, wet, soft. Burton's eyes were open. 'C'mon you Scottish twat, you fuckin' stay with me, you fuckin' stay with me.' Jimmy twisted and shouted, 'Medic' again, then back to Burton he whispered, 'You fuckin' stay with me, got that?'

Burton's eyes seemed to focus on Jimmy's face. Then they milked over and became sightless and his chest heaved for the last time.

Leach had to pull Jimmy away. He was still screaming for the medics and applying CPR to him when the Colonel rushed up behind him and saw what was happening.

'Vickers, Vickers, he's dead man, dead,' Leach said, hauling Jimmy up under the armpits and dragging him away from the body to let in a medical crew. 'He's dead, James … you gotta let him go, man,' Leach said.

Jimmy looked down at his blood-soaked hands and arms.

***

Two hours later, he walked numbly into Leach's office and sat down opposite his boss, who regarded him thoughtfully.

Leach could see some psychological cracks in Jimmy, but there wasn't the time to address these now – or ever, maybe. For the moment, there was business to be done.

'The Taliban you shot in the shoulder ... still alive, being treated in the hospital as we speak.'

Jimmy raised his eyes.

'He and his fellow Taliban fooled us for a long, long time – and because of that, six good British soldiers and two loyal Afghan servicemen have been murdered in cold blood today.'

Jimmy said nothing, but inside, something surged.

'At present there are over two hundred Afghan soldiers billeted with us at Bastion and the fear is that more infiltrators will be among them. I want you to speak to the injured man and extract any information he has about those others embedded. We think there's a good chance he has this knowledge.'

A light came on in Jimmy's eyes, a reaction noted by Leach.

'I appreciate what you've just been through, Vickers, but although time is of the essence, I do need you to maintain some objectivity in your task ... so channel your emotions into that and use any methods you have at your disposal. I don't need to tell you, you know the limits.'

Jimmy nodded, started to rise from the chair.

'And just for the record, I, too, am devastated by what happened to Mickey Burton. He was a good soldier, a valuable member of this team and a good friend.'

'Amen,' Jimmy thought.

***

Jimmy Vickers could not differentiate between the sources of the pounding. Was it in his head, or was it the rifle butts smashing at the door of the hospital store room? Was it the blood pulsating through his temples or the crashing of the feet of the soldiers trying to kick down the door?

Whichever, he would never know.

What was for certain was that he had dragged the injured Taliban from his hospital bed, the drip stands crashing around him as the needles were ripped out of his veins, blood spitting everywhere, the blood pressure and heartbeat monitors dragged off their stands as Jimmy tore the pads off the man's chest and then, not even hearing the petrified screaming of the nurses and the shouted orders of the doctors, Jimmy had physically dragged him down a corridor and into a store room which he locked from the inside, and then barricaded himself in – with his prisoner.

As an opener, Jimmy had turned on the frightened man, pulled the dressing off the shoulder wound and inserted his right thumb deep into the bullet hole, through flesh and muscle, grinding the end of it on the shoulder socket, finding the nerves, making the man shriek.

'Talk to me, you fucker, talk to me,' Jimmy growled.

And he did.

The next certain thing was that before the soldiers managed to burst through the door and clamber over the barricade, their weapons aimed at Jimmy, the Taliban lay dead at his feet.

But the pounding, pulsating noise continued.

***

Jimmy woke with a start, cradling his head, allowing the noise to subside. He opened his eyes, looked around his cell. Swinging his legs out, he sat up on the metal framed camp bed.

'Shit,' he breathed and walked over to the toilet, scooping out some water from the bowl and dousing himself. He was steaming hot and sweat poured from him.

It was his second week in custody, and the preliminary hearing before his elders and betters was due to take place later today. Despite the manoeuvrings and influence of Colonel Leach, Jimmy's future was very much in the balance, because what had happened to the Taliban warrior had happened in public, and his unit was struggling to control things because other people – doctors, nurses, orderlies, other soldiers – were involved.

Jimmy had lost it through grief, taken it one step too far, and now too many people were in the loop, nit picking, demanding answers, asking questions, and it was becoming an embarrassing bureaucratic nightmare – and because of all that, Jimmy had clammed up, said nothing, refused to divulge anything the Taliban had admitted to him.

He heard the key turn in the cell door.

It opened; Colonel Leach stood there, his frame virtually filling the door. This was the man who had been Jimmy's father figure and mentor, who had developed Jimmy's skills and character and was also ruthless in their use.

Jimmy knew it was only 4am. He didn't have a watch, but the rhythms of Camp Bastion were ingrained in him and he could tell the time just from the feel of the day.

'Boss?' Jimmy said, frowning. Leach had been to see him numerous times over the past two weeks – but never at four in the morning.

The dark expression on Leach's normally implacable countenance told Jimmy this was not one of those routine visits.

++++

ONE

LONDON

They swarmed into the shop, fast, hard and ruthless, like a pack of rabid wolves. Three of them, all young men – of course – two brandishing handguns, a third wielding a baseball bat. They had picked their time well, with no other customers in Dalvinder's little pawn shop, just the owner and his wife; they came in at the most vulnerable moment they could, clearly having kept the shop under observation beforehand. They struck just as the owner stepped out from behind the security counter onto the shop floor and started to help his wife rearrange the window display.

It could not have been better timed. These boys were good.

They moved initially in a coordinated manner, knowing their roles: one at the door to prevent any customer straying into the robbery, one to the husband, one to the wife. Screaming violently from behind their distorted masks that were demonic versions of Prime Minister David Cameron's face.

The wife – Mrs Dalvinder – was easy to subdue. She was a small Asian woman, dressed midway between India and east London, a sort of hybrid get up, a long, flowing silk scarf around her neck which the robber grabbed and wrapped around her neck three more times as he heaved tight and wrenched the woman down, kneeing her hard in the side of her head while screwing the muzzle of his Russian automatic pistol into her neck and forcing her face into the tiled floor.

The husband, too, was a slightly built man in his sixties, wearing an open necked shirt and trousers, and he was marched by the largest member of the gang – who held him easily by the collar, with his gun rammed hard into the base of his spine – behind the security counter where the safe, till and the most recent acquisitions of the shop were located.

Mr Dalvinder followed the instructions that were screamed at him and, with visibly shaking hands, he emptied the contents of the till into the supermarket carrier bag provided by the robber, maybe a thousand pounds, give or take, in mixed notes. Then, with the gun at the back of his head, he crouched down at the safe under the counter and unlocked it, tapping in the code on the key pad before a green light came on and it opened with a little clunk to reveal the contents.

That was the moment Dalvinder made the decision that cost him his life. The moment when he knew that if he handed over the contents of the safe to this young, wild man, his business could not survive the loss. His money was stacked deep and high within the little safe, together with a couple of small, drawstring silk sachets containing loose diamonds and other valuable gemstones he had acquired over the years. When he eventually decided to sell them on, it would bring him and his family many thousands of pounds. Retirement money.

He turned his head and looked into the eyes behind that terrifying mask.

And the young man knew the pawnbroker had decided to defy him.

A very stupid decision, but before the robber could warn him not to be brave, Dalvinder had lurched towards the under counter foot button that triggered the alarm. The young man knew it was audible and that it was also connected directly to an alarm company whose headquarters were in Hounslow. He knew this because he had done his homework. He also knew that within moments of the alarm lighting up the panel at the company's operating centre, the police would be alerted. If there were any patrols out there, they would be at the shop within minutes.

The masked man lost all control at that point.

The drugs and adrenaline pulsating through his system, plus the intense excitement of the moment – the high of committing an armed robbery – made him kick out with the flat of his foot against the side of Dalvinder's head, sending the small man sprawling behind the counter.

But then he could not stop, the floodgates had opened.

He kicked Dalvinder's head remorselessly, stomped on him and then, finally, pumped two bullets into his chest and one into his head.

He scooped up the carrier bag, crammed it with the money from the safe, not caring about the sachets because dealing with gems was not his thing. Then he turned, glancing up at the CCTV camera positioned high and unreachable behind a wire mesh on the ceiling.

He stopped – just for a moment – and arrogantly aimed the gun at the lens, but then he was gone.

He ran out, stepping over Mrs Dalvinder's prostrate form, and cruelly used her body to propel himself, shouting for his mates to get out of the shop.

And they were gone, leaving death in their wake.

***

PC Tony Griffin – Griff – swallowed hard, his eyes cold. He pressed the pause button on the old VHS video cassette recorder on which grainy images of the robbery had been captured on a tape that had probably been used a thousand times. It was linked to two CCTV cameras in Dalvinder's shop, recording a split image – one behind the counter and one with a wider view of the shop floor.

Griff had watched the gang enter the shop, then the whole of the robbery unfold.

The terrified Mrs Dalvinder being held down on the floor while her husband had been bundled behind the counter and then, probably less than a minute later (Griff hadn't timed it yet, but he would) shot dead. It had happened very quickly.

Griff paused the tape at the moment the robber had pointed his gun at the camera, while in the background lay the unmoving body of Mr Dalvinder, put down like a dog.

The paused image on the screen juddered unsteadily, lines of interference and wear and tear across the much-used tape. Griff tried to look into the eyes of the killer. But all he could see were two pitch black eyes of nothingness. Griff's mouth twitched.

He pressed play again and the lad was gone, and all that filled the half-screen then was the dead man, blood pouring out from the head wound and pooling blackly underneath him. Then Mrs Dalvinder crossed from one side of the split screen to the other as she crawled from the shop floor behind the counter, where she saw her husband and came up on her knees, and covered her face with her hands at the horror of the image.

A tragedy enacted in seconds, a life taken, a life destroyed.

Griff rewound the tape to the beginning of the robbery, teeing it up and then pressing stop so that it would be ready for re-watching by other officers. He stood up on dithery legs, his own adrenaline surge having subsided, leaving him feeling weak and with a petrol-like taste in his mouth.

He walked to the office door and looked along the tight corridor back to the shop, where he could see Dalvinder's body, not yet having been moved other than minutely by the police surgeon who had formally pronounced life extinct.

It was an obvious diagnosis, but one that had to be formalised.

Now the body lay there, uncovered, for the crime scene and forensic investigation teams to do their work of recording and evidence collection.

Griff swallowed that petrol taste again as he took in the scene.

He stepped into the corridor and turned the opposite direction to the shop, into the living accommodation at the back of the property where the Dalvinder family lived. Griff knew they had been in business in this location for twenty-plus years. They were well known and respected in the community.

Before entering the living room, he smoothed down the front of the white forensic suit he was wearing over his uniform and tapped lightly to announce his presence, then entered.

It was a room full of dated furniture, carpets and wallpaper, having a very 1960s feel to it.

Mrs Dalvinder sat on the edge of an armchair, hunched over her knees, constantly running a handkerchief through her fingers and dabbing her wet, blood-shot eyes and dripping nose with it.

Directly opposite her, sitting face to face, knee to knee, on the corner of a dining chair, was Jenny Clarke, a young policewoman, one of Griff's colleagues, working out of the same police station, covering the same area. She too was wearing a forensic suit over her uniform. But it was far too large for her and billowed out. Clarke glanced at Griff. She was a very pretty lady, but at that moment her features were drawn tight and she looked exhausted at having to deal with the grief and death.

Just another day in the Met, Griff thought sourly.

Clarke gave her head a tiny shake, indicating she was getting very little from the grieving widow. Her expression was one of helplessness.

Griff tilted his head. Clarke touched Mrs Dalvinder's shoulder reassuringly and whispered something, getting a nod back, then stood up and crossed to Griff who drew her out into the corridor.

'Anything?' he asked.

'She's traumatised,' Clarke said quietly. 'Basically, just witnessed her husband being executed in front of her eyes, Griff.'

He nodded, understanding.

Clarke touched her personal radio. 'DCI's on his way,' she said. 'ETA about now.'

Griff nodded again. 'I'll just have a quick word with her, if you don't mind?'

Clarke shrugged. 'Be my guest. She's a wreck and it doesn't help that English is her second language.'

'I know.' The two shared a look and Griff entered the room, feeling despair on so many levels. He took up the position vacated by Clarke, his knees virtually touching Mrs Dalvinder's, but not quite. 'Mrs Dalvinder,' he spoke softly, 'I know it's really hard, but it is important that we gather as much evidence as soon as we can. That gives us a much, much better chance of catching these…' Griff's lips tightened on the word, '…people.'

'The one at the door … black and white hoodie,' she said, talking through the streaming tears. 'It was so fast, so quick.'

'It's okay,' Griff said and sighed. He sat upright as a new face appeared at the living room door and he was beckoned out by the man.

Griff crumbled slightly inside.

The DCI had arrived.

He stood up wearily and joined him in the corridor, only to find the sharp-suited man concentrating on sending a text from his state-of-the-art mobile phone. He glanced at Griff and said, 'One sec, mate.' He pressed send, grinned, then slid the phone into a pocket and gave Griff some attention.

Detective Chief Inspector Spencer Holland was still on the better side of thirty-five, with a fast moving but less than illustrious career behind him – that is, if any of the cops he'd come across out on the streets had been asked for their opinion (they weren't) – and looked to have much the same ahead of him. He fully expected to be a superintendent by thirty-eight, chief super by forty-two and then right up in the higher echelons of assistant commissioner level well before the fifty mark. He was a man on an accelerating trajectory, and this particular stop – as DCI at Griff's nick – was one of those minor but necessary blips. Another line on an already overcrowded CV.

'Okay,' Holland said briskly, 'what've we got, PC..?'

'Griffin.'

'PC Griffin … need to remember that. Look, I'm due to tee off with the super at one and I don't need to be late because of this shit.' Holland spun and walked towards Dalvinder's body. Griff could hardly believe that Holland hadn't even put on a forensic suit, the absolutely necessary clothing for a serious crime scene. He could imagine Holland hustling past the poor PC on the door, whose job it was to record all comings and goings and issue the suits. Holland still had on his fucking lounge suit and polished brogues. 'So,' Holland said over his shoulder as he dropped into a squat near to Dalvinder's head, making sure his shiny shoes did not touch any blood or brain matter. 'You were first on the scene?'

'Yeah.'

He had expected more words from Griff. They didn't come.

'And?' he demanded belligerently.

'Armed robbery. Three offenders. All masked. Mr Dalvinder looks like he might have tried to set off the alarm, got shot for trying and they got away with the contents of the till and money from the safe.'

Holland picked up something from the floor, held it up between his thumb and forefinger. It twinkled. A diamond. 'Maybe not just cash,' he commented.

'Looks like a bag of diamonds spilled,' Griff observed.

Both raised their eyes as Jenny Clarke came to the end of the corridor, clearly not expecting to see Holland down on his haunches.

She said a quick sorry for interrupting and backed away.

'That's a tidy bit of business,' Holland commented inappropriately and slyly to Griff. He placed the diamond back on the floor and rose up to his full height, shaking his head. 'CCTV?' He glanced at the camera.

'Yeah – but it's dated. VHS. A very old tape, poor picture quality but just about watchable. Black and white. Clearly see they had masks on, though. Sort of distorted David Cameron things.'

'Good luck finding them, then,' Holland smirked. He shook his head again and looked at Dalvinder's shattered head, the blood now coagulating like black tar underneath him. 'What's he doing being a brave fucker?'

'I don't know … protecting his livelihood?' Griff suggested, feeling an incredible anger and resentment towards this man.

'Livelihood? This? You serious?' Holland turned, gesturing with the palms of his hands.

'It matters to them,' Griff said.

'I'm sure it does, PC..? Sorry, I forget.'

'Griffin.'

Holland stepped conspiratorially towards Griff and lowered his voice. 'Look – it's probably an insurance scam gone bad. Try not to take it too personally, mate,' he said like a condescending big brother. 'The wife'll make a claim, big pay out – Kerching! – everyone's happy.'

Holland patted Griff on the shoulder just as his phone beeped to announce an incoming text. He fished it out of his pocket and thumbed through the keys to bring up the message, which he read with a smirk on his face.

Griff stared at him with complete disapproval. 'And the suspects? The offenders?'

Holland had started to write a reply to the text, his concentration nowhere near Griff. He scowled, 'Er … get the bullets out of Hardeep Bronson once he gets to the mortuary and get 'em sent off to ballistics.' He pressed 'send' and grinned. 'It'll obviously take some time but, hey, slow justice is better than no justice. That's what I say.'

Another patronising pat on the shoulder, then he whirled away, steeping carefully over Dalvinder, and made his way out of the shop, humming brightly to himself.

'That guy's heading this murder investigation?'

Griff turned. Somehow PC Clarke had managed to make her way up behind him.

'Yeah,' Griff said dully, watching the DCI's back.

'How the hell ..?'

'Plays the game … wins the game.'

'And where the hell does justice fit into that?' Clarke demanded.

'It doesn't,' Griff said. 'Let's get this scene properly sorted.'

++++

TWO

Even now, thirty-five years down the line. George Vickers still gave silent thanks to Sandra Daniels, the girl who had saved his life.

As ever – old habits – George opened his eyes a minute before his alarm went off at 6.45am. He reached out and flicked the button to the off position and lay back for a moment, rubbing his eyes that were gritty and getting old. Then he looked sideways at Sandra, still sleeping soundly – which amazed George because of the intense personal pressure both of them were under each day. George hid his feelings under a mask of male bravado, but Sandra wore her heart on her sleeve and George was happy about that. They each had a different way of dealing with the fact that their son, their one and only child – although he was no longer a child – was fighting in a war thousands of miles away in a scorching desert and against a merciless enemy.

But for that moment in time, as George gazed at the woman who had become his wife over thirty years ago, all he could think about was her, still so utterly beautiful … and his heart pounded just a few beats harder at the great life they'd had together.

He knew he shouldn't – Sandra loved the extra fifteen minutes in bed when he got out and she took the opportunity to spread and doze – but George couldn't resist. He leaned carefully across, took her gorgeous, heart shaped face in the palms of his hands and kissed her closed eyelids tenderly.

She stirred and smiled. 'Mornin' lover,' she murmured, as if they were both still teenage sweethearts.

'You too,' he said, slightly cross with himself for having disturbed her. He rolled out of bed and tiptoed into the shower room, thinking that he moved with the silence of a panther.

Sandra watched him disappear into the en suite, unable to stop herself from grinning. Then she checked the time and saw she had ten minutes more, so she huddled deeper under the duvet and closed her eyes, but only for a moment. They opened again and she sat up, eyeing the door to the en suite, hearing the rumble of the shower beyond. She picked up her mobile phone from the bedside cabinet, needing to make a call which she knew would probably not be answered.

***

Despite the early rise, breakfast was always a rush. For Sandra, anyway. George was showered and shaved in ten minutes, dressed five minutes later and in the kitchen immediately after that. While he prepared breakfast, he could hear Sandra scuttling around upstairs above him.

Another habit of a lifetime, George always made himself a cooked breakfast, whereas he laid out the muesli, yogurt and honey that constituted Sandra's morning meal. That, plus the pot of coffee they always shared.

She bustled into the kitchen, adjusting her hair and applying her lipstick.

'Forgot I had a curriculum meeting at eight-fifteen,' she said breathlessly. Sandra worked at a local college where she now headed up a department. It was a job that George didn't really understand, but he was immensely proud of the success she'd had and was happy to play a supporting role for her.

'Mornin' to you, too,' he teased her.

'Bye!'

She tiptoed over and pecked him on the cheek, cheekily pinched a sausage from his plate, then spun away to leave.

'Hang on,' George said, mock-affronted.

'I'm late, George,' she said, pulling on her jacket as she got to the back door, where she stopped and turned back. 'Ooh … I'll be back late, too. Can you mow the lawn?'

'Why?'

She dropped her shoulders and gave him one of those withering, 'Are you stupid?' expressions. 'Jimmy's coming home. I want to start making the place look nice.'

'It'll have grown back by then,' George remonstrated. He forked half a sausage – the only one he had left on his plate – and stuffed it into his mouth. Sandra shrugged herself into her jacket and buttoned it up.

'Yeah, but it's gonna rain all week after today and we both know it'll never get done.' She patted down her pockets, then foraged in her handbag, muttering and when she looked up she saw that George was dangling her car keys enticingly from his fingers. She gave an exasperated gasp.

'He's been in the Afghan desert for months, darlin'. The last thing he's gonna care about is an uncut lawn. He might like to see a bit of greenery.'

Sandra snatched the keys and looked at them in the palm of her hand, catching sight of the photograph in the clear plastic fob. It stopped her in her tracks, and George noticed this.

'All right, love?'

He knew what had struck her, what had caused her to take a moment out of her rush. A faded photograph of her, proudly holding a new born Jimmy in her arms. She looked drained but exhilarated. George had snapped it only minutes after the birth and the photo had been with Sandra every day since, from car to car.

'Just wish he'd come home for good, y'know?' she said wistfully.

George nodded understanding. He took hold of her hand and angled her palm so he could see the photograph he knew so well.

His son, his lad. He had to swallow hard at that moment and blink away his emotion, and to do so he had to bluster with humour. 'You look a right mess in that picture, you know?' He said it, but didn't mean it. He thought she had looked the most beautiful he had ever seen her, as exhausted as she was.

She batted him playfully, their eyes meeting.

'I'd been in labour for seven hours! Lucky you were behind the lens, otherwise we'd be laughing at your mullet and ear ring. Talk about a mess.'

George was still holding her hand, the clear memory of those times flooding back. 'One minute we were bombing about on the back of a bike, next we'd got a son. Didn't know what hit us, did we?'

'At ten-thirty that night I knew exactly what hit us.'

Their eyes were still locked. 'I'll mow the lawn when I get home.'

'Thanks love.'

George rose from the breakfast table and they embraced tenderly and as Sandra pulled away he saw a lone tear roll down her cheek. He thumbed it away in a particularly intimate gesture. 'He'll be okay, y'know.'

She nodded, tiptoed up for a second peck on the cheek, turned and left.

***

As it happened, George was unable to mow the lawn that evening because he'd forgotten that as ever, on a Thursday, the shop he worked in opened late.

It was not George's dream job to work behind the counter in Cash4Gold. His ambition early in life had been to be a boxer and in some respects, the East End of London, where he was born and bred, was an ideal place to make that dream come true. Up to the age of twenty, there had been a good chance of turning professional, but George had taken a bad eye injury one night in a London gym from a particularly brutal Puerto Rican fighter, who almost took out George's left eye with a punch and an illegal twist. George had proceeded to pound his opponent into the mat, blood flecking everywhere, but the injury which damaged his eye tissue meant that boxing was no longer an option or even a possibility. Medical reasons banned him from the ring – but in reality he had always known that although he had skill and courage, he didn't have that certain "something" that set the best boxers at a level above all the other wannabes.

The time following the eye injury had been the toughest months of his life, and he could easily have gravitated down to East End gangland. Handy boys like George were much sought after as enforcers and punishers and he was courted by a number of crime bosses.

If it hadn't been for the appearance in his life of Sandra Daniels, a teacher in training, whom he met one particularly bad day in a pub in central London, he would have succumbed to 'the life'. He had started drinking heavily to drown his disappointments over the eye injury and career that would never be and he was on the cusp of a job with a man who ran girls and drugs on the edge of Soho.

That Sandra saw something decent, honest and upright in him was something for which he was thankful to this day.

They clicked. He cleaned up his act, and the next pint of beer he had was on Jimmy's eighteenth birthday, when the lad took his old dad out for a bevy. Though George did spend time in his local, the only occasions on which he drank alcohol were with his son.

Although George never had Sandra's intellect, he did have a propensity for hard work and became a moderately successful property developer after Sandra had pointed him in the direction of some basic qualifications relating to the building trade.

Then came marriage and the boy, James.

And George became completely focused on his home life and the upbringing of a son.

He had never looked back.

Except that in his mid-forties his back had gone and he had to leave the building trade and had somehow ended up behind the counter of Cash4Gold because the owner needed someone with presence but who was also approachable, friendly and trustworthy. George ticked all those boxes.

But yes, it wasn't his ideal job, particularly as the recession bit and more and more people were forced to swap valuable heirlooms or jewellery with sentimental connections for cold hard cash in order to survive.

George always paid the best prices he could, but even so it sometimes broke his heart to see old people having to part with wedding or engagement rings.

'Too bloody soft,' he often chided himself.

***

Darkness had come.

The narrow alley was blocked by the tatty red Ford Focus, no room either side to squeeze by. Anyone passing the end of the alley and glancing down would have been able to see four shapes in the car, with the occasional spit of brightness as the young men inside handed their rolled up cigarettes and crack pipe between them.

The front passenger snorted a line of coke from a mirror – one of four lines – then passed it onto the lad next to him behind the wheel, who took his turn, then passed the mirror over his shoulder to the guys behind. Just a line each.

Coke, crack, Red Bull, tobacco, Lucozade.

They were bubbling now, ready.

The driver's name was Rob. He reached to the CD player and cranked up the volume of the bass/drum track, and started to move to the rhythm. But not too loud. They didn't want any undue attention being paid to them.

Danny was the one in the front passenger seat. At his feet was a black sports bag.

He reached into it and took out the first weapon, passing it into the first hand that grabbed it from the back seat; then the next, then the one sideways to Rob. The names of the lads in the back were Josh and Leon.

Each cocked their weapons.

Their familiarity with them was all too scary, especially in their drugged up, hyper state. Releasing magazine clips from the pistol grips, checking to see if they were fully loaded, then slotting them back and cocking the slides. Serious weapons.

'We ready boys?' Rob asked.

'We ready,' came the chorus.

'Then we go.'

The last thing they did was pull on their David Cameron masks. Rob gunned the car out of the alley, screeching around ninety degrees and accelerating the hundred or so yards to their target premises: Cash4Gold.

***

'A cage fighter, ey?' George eyed the individual standing in front of him across the counter. He was a well-toned lad with well-defined muscles, tanned from a bottle and a sunbed, his thick blonde hair slicked back and an arrogant look on his face.

'Soft as shit,' George thought. He wouldn't last two rounds with some of the up and coming boxers he knew. But then again, those lads probably wouldn't be able to handle sliding around in a cage, covered in baby oil, being gawped at by drunken, hyped-up night clubbers. The thought sickened George. As a form of entertainment he found it tasteless and crude, a million miles distant from the regal sport he loved.

'That'ths right pal,' the lad lisped.

'Good for you ... so what've you got?'

He swung a backpack off his shoulders onto the counter and unzipped the side pocket, pulling out a chain of thick gold. 'Thith.'

George hefted the jewellery in the palm of his hand, his bottom lip pouting thoughtfully, already knowing this was the real deal, serious bling. Even so, this was the sort of punter that George didn't mind driving a hard bargain with.

'It'th pure gold,' the cage fighter said.

'Yeah,' George agreed.

***

They steamed in through the front door of the shop, howling terrible threats, waving their weapons, and although the shop was a reasonable size, Rob was at the counter instantly, vaulting over it like a trained athlete, a short knife in his right hand, his pistol in his left, and barging George back against the wall ... George had tripped the silent alarm the moment the front door had burst open and the gang had surged in.

'Where's your fuckin' safe, old man, your fuckin' safe?' Rob screamed into George's face, spitting as he shouted, holding the knife under George's chin.

Stood covering them a few feet further back, bouncing from foot to foot, was Josh. He jerked his gun up and down, unable to keep it still or stop his forefinger from wrapping and unwrapping itself around the trigger.

George took all this in and the fact that the two other gang members, both armed with baseball bats, had started smashing the glass fronted display cabinets on the shop floor like they were demented.

The cage fighter backed away in terror, almost crying. He took the chance to snatch his gold chain off the counter, turned and fled screaming from the shop.

'I said, where's your safe?' Rob snarled right into George's face.

'Fuck you,' George responded defiantly, showing no fear.

Rob crashed his right fist hard into the side of George's jaw, sending him spinning. As he steadied himself on the counter, Rob drove the knife hard down into the back of George's outspread hand, then jerked it free.

George howled and clamped his bleeding hand against his chest, suddenly realising that he may well be too old to deal with these bastards. He was not quick enough, not dangerous enough any more – and this gang clearly meant business.

'In the back, in the back,' George said.

Rob swung him around and force-marched him ahead, jamming his gun into George's back, gesturing for Josh to come along with them. Rob, with George in front, clutching his injured hand, moved into the tiny office at the back of the shop where a digital safe sat on a shelf, screwed to the wall. Out of the corner of his eye, George saw the only bit of personal protection that the shop had – a baseball bat – leaning against the desk.

Rob slid the muzzle of the gun into George's neck, twisting it hard, almost screwing it into his skin, making George gasp with pain.

'Open the fucker.'

George typed in the code and as he did, the two gang members slid up their masks, knowing there was no camera in this room. They were sweating heavily, eyes blazing with satisfaction and they smiled ferociously at each other. Brothers in Arms, fighting a campaign together.

The safe opened and Rob shoved George out of the way, pinning him up against the wall with his forearm.

Josh stepped across to the safe door and gazed in at the massive stash of notes, all neatly bound. His chin dropped. 'Fuck me,' he said incredulously. 'Jackpot.'

'C'mon man, just bag it, don't fuck about, just bag it,' Rob yelled and stepped away from George to urge on Josh, who was pulling a plastic supermarket carrier bag from his pocket.

That was the moment George saw his chance. Although he knew he was being rash and foolhardy, brave or stupid, he was livid and pride rushed through him. He did not want these young men to be walking out of here with that money.

As Rob stepped back and looked at Josh, whose face was right up to the safe door, George pushed him hard.

Caught off guard by George's unexpected speed and surge of power, he stumbled back against the opposite wall, giving George just the time and space he needed to reach down and grab the baseball bat. He swung it round and it crashed down onto Rob's gun wrist. The weapon clattered to the floor as the pain shot up the entire length of his arm.

George kicked the weapon away and went for Rob again, but Rob had got himself together. He ducked underneath the arcing bat and threw himself out of the office.

Josh was slower to react, but George's blood was now pulsing and he raised the bat like he was some sort of medieval knight and whacked it hard against the side of Josh's left knee. His leg crumbled and he went down as George whipped the bat around and smacked Josh's gun out of his hand, kicking it out into the corridor.

George went after Rob, who had fled back into the store, pulled down his mask and slithered across the counter top, screaming, 'Go, let's go,' to the other two.

Leon and Danny read him instantly: something had gone wrong back there. They went for the door with bags already bulging with looted goods from the display cases.

George wasn't far behind Rob now. He too went over the counter, but without the grace and speed of the much lighter Rob. And behind him was Josh, dragging his injured leg and holding his sore hand.

That was the moment of the next decision for George.

Cut his losses and take one of the gang as his prisoner, hold him until the cops landed, or chase and probably lose the rest of the gang.

It was a no brainer.

George came up short and turned his attention to Josh, stepping between him and the door, the only means of escape.

Josh computed this, reached into his pocket and pulled out a flick knife which clicked open. 'I will go through you, you old cunt.'

George stood his ground. One attacker – a slip of a lad for all his bravado and toughness – even with a knife did not worry him. This one would be easy and George slapped the head of the baseball bat into the palm of his hand. He stared coldly at Josh.

But in the heat and flurry and confusion of it all, George had assumed that the three others had fled.

He was wrong.

Rob had stopped in the doorway, turned and closed the door.

George spun and saw him – and the long-bladed knife held loosely down at his thigh. George suddenly realised he was sandwiched and would have to retreat again, something that made him shudder with revulsion. God, if he'd only been twenty years younger, these guys would all be flat out now.

Suddenly Josh lunged at him from behind, a blur of movement that George saw just in the periphery of his vision.

Instinctively he swung back. The baseball bat travelled through the air, making a whooshing noise. It wasn't an aimed, deliberate blow, just a defensive move – but even so it connected with a horrible echoing sound which was the combination of the shockwave through the wood of the bat itself and what it struck. Josh's head whipped around, taking the full force of the blow. He sank back against the counter and slumped to the floor.

George moved back and stood over him, the adrenaline in his system fuelling everything now.

He screamed at Rob. 'You come and get him. I dare you to come and get him.' His voice rose even higher. 'Well come on.'

Rob eyeballed George from behind the mask, relishing this. This is what he did, what he was good at. Violence. It was his world, part of the currency traded in the subculture he lived in.

He took a threatening step, but then halted, cocking his head slightly. Sirens in the distance, getting louder, cops on the way.

Time to go. Josh would just have to handle what came.

Rob raised his knife and pointed it at George, the gesture unmistakeable in its meaning: we are not through.

Then he was gone.

George stood there, breathing heavily. He half-expected Rob to return, but it didn't happen. As quickly as the adrenaline had pulsated into his system, it was gone, leaving George deflated, empty and dithery.

He turned, expecting one more confrontation, but his expression changed to one of horror when he realised that the youth he'd struck with the bat had not moved since dropping to the floor and that blood was oozing slowly across the floor from the deep gash on the lad's head.

George stooped and felt for a pulse in his neck.

There was none.

++++

THREE

The words being spoken were only just going into George's brain, being sluggishly understood but not responded to.

He was in the back room of the laundrette next door to the Cash4Gold shop, having been led there in a trance by the manageress of the business.

He sat hunched forward, staring blankly at the floor, in deep shock, desperately trying to make sense of what had happened. His lips moved silently, speaking unheard words to himself, his head shaking slightly from side to side, his face a series of tics and frowns as he relived the moments gone.

He looked up. 'Sorry?'

The questions had been asked softly by PC Jenny Clarke who was fast becoming experienced at dealing with all forms of grief.

George took in Clarke's pretty young face, already etched with lines from the sharp end of policing.

'Sorry,' he said again absently, her words having drifted over him.

'...And then he came at you from behind..?'

George blanked off again.

***

Behind the counter of Cash4Gold, Griff watched a replay of the incident on the shop's CCTV system, a much better quality system than the one in the pawnshop a week ago. Better quality, same scenario, Griff thought glumly, using the remote control to flick back and forth through the horrific images on the monitor affixed to the wall at the back of the counter. He then thought cynically, 'Another day, same shit times ten.' A point of view reinforced as the front door of the shop opened and DCI Spencer Holland strutted cockily into the scene.

Griff's heart gave a dull thud in his chest. He watched Holland barge his way through the CSIs to the dead boy on the floor, doing a Fred Astaire sidestep to keep his expensive shoes out of the blood.

He gave Griff a knowing wink, then bent down to lift the corner of the plastic sheet now covering Josh's inert form. He grimaced, shook his head and looked at Griff.

'Same crew,' Griff said, gesturing with the remote control at the monitor. 'One more of them, but the same boys. Cameron masks. Very bad lads.'

'Now one less of 'em,' Holland quipped. His face scrunched up.

'Got what he asked for … I know George Vickers, the guy who did it, and he's not like that.'

'Not like what? Not like someone who thinks he has a right to do this sort of thing, have an offensive weapon to hand just in case?'

'They had guns and knives and bats,' Griff said, suddenly feeling very bad about this, and not just because someone had died … for a whole different reason, one called Spencer Holland.

'Did they actually use 'em?' Holland said, standing upright. 'Or did the old guy simply take the law into his own hands? I've actually heard a bit about George Vickers. Used to be a tough guy in these parts, so they say.' Holland turned away, leaving Griff astounded. 'Let's go see exactly how tough an old bird he is.'

****

Clarke thought she was making progress. Eliciting good information from traumatised people was a skill that took time to hone and the practice of that skill needed patience, sympathy, empathy and some degree of firmness. She had coaxed George into talking a little, got him to explain the robbery and she was asking questions to follow this up so she could make sense of things, get what happened in order and then, only then, would she take a written statement. She was thorough and, as her career progressed, getting very good at her job.

'… And then he came at you from behind..?'

George considered the question, squinting as he thought back, trying to recall it accurately. A paramedic now knelt in front of him, dressing the knife wound in his hand which would need to be seen at a hospital in due course.

He thought back, squinting, trying to piece it together: the action he had taken, how he had reacted, how he felt ... but the moment of reflection was shattered by the appearance of DCI Holland, who swung into the room on the door jamb, his right hand extended as he held out his warrant card.

'I just wanted to stop him...' George had begun.

Holland interrupted. 'DCI Holland, officer in charge of this investigation.'

'I never meant...' George continued.

'Well perhaps you should have thought of that before you started swinging your bat around like a cave man,' Holland cut in.

George stared open-mouthed at him.

Holland's own mouth closed in a cruel, contemptuous, thin-lipped line. His head turned slowly from George to Clarke and he spoke rudely to her as though George wasn't even there, as if he was unimportant. 'Let's get him out of here for further questioning, get his hand seen to if we have to. Need to move quick ... as soon as word gets round this neighbourhood about this, we'll have a lynch mob down here if we're not careful.' He raised his eyebrows. 'You know what they're like round here.' To George, he said, 'You're gonna have to come with us.'

'How serious is this?'

Holland shook his head sadly. 'Duh – about as serious as it gets. I'm arresting you on suspicion of murder. You do not have to say anything, but it may harm your defence if you do not mention when questioned something which you later rely on in court. Anything you do say may be given in evidence.'

As he spoke, George focused in on Holland's mouth, but the words coming out of it seemed distorted and unreal.

***

The custody sergeant handed George back the last of his property, put his finger on the prisoner's property sheet, indicating where George had to sign to acknowledge its return. George signed with his left hand, his right now bandaged and treated following a trip to A&E while under arrest.

'And this is a copy of the police bail form,' the sergeant said.

George nodded, took it distractedly and folded it into four.

'Back in two weeks,' the sergeant said.

'I know.'

The sergeant regarded George with sympathy but said nothing about his predicament. He pointed, 'Out of that door and you'll be in the waiting room ... someone's there for you.'

Still in a deep haze, George walked to the exit, was buzzed through and into the waiting area.

Sandra shot up the instant he came through the door, rushed to meet him and they hugged each other tightly, clinging for many seconds, Sandra uttering, 'Oh George, George ... they wouldn't let me see you.'

'It's okay darling.' He stroked her hair.

'Oh God, I was so worried.'

George held her gently away, bent slightly and looked into the depths of her eyes. He had regained some of his composure – albeit tinged with disbelief. 'It'll be all right, Sandra. They're just going through the motions. They have to. Someone died,' – he almost choked on the word as the enormity of the situation struck him, again. 'They have to investigate it properly ... it's what they do.'

'If you say so.' She did not sound convinced.

'I say so ... and Jimmy'll be home soon, he'll know what to do, so c'mon, let's get home. I need to be there right now.'

***

They were silent – and not a little terrified – as they walked along the corridor. The three remnants of the robbery crew, Rob, Leon and Danny, following the huge muscled man who was the guardian of this, the top floor of the tower block that had been taken over and fortified by Warren Evans and his partner in crime, Caleb Brown. These two young men virtually controlled a wide swathe of crime in this particular borough of east London from this location, which also doubled as Caleb's home. Drugs were their main source of income but they also robbed to order, ran protection rackets and, more and more, trafficked women as prostitutes from all across the globe – which was proving to be the most profitable and least risky line of all.

This criminal empire was not the reason why the three were afraid.

Their fear was for a whole different reason.

The security man held up a very muscled arm: stop. They had reached the door which led into the flat. And from this side it looked just a normal door to a normal flat.

It wasn't.

Behind this door was the headquarters of Warren and Caleb's criminal enterprise. Three flats, side by side, had been acquired and knocked through, and few people knew, or wanted to know, what went on inside. That was the kind of knowledge that could cause pain – or even death – and was best avoided. But the three young men knew that beyond this door was a rabbit warren of rooms, three two-bedroomed flats knocked together, interconnected. They included a small gym, a cinema projection room, three very plush bedrooms, plus a couple of other box rooms used by any friends who might have to lay low, and a large living room that few people ever saw. Most of Warren and Caleb's lives were led from this domain, although Warren did not actually live here. But it was from this ivory tower of security that they planned their operations and dispatched their foot soldiers to carry out their bidding and then return with the fruits of their labour – which was usually money, sometimes gold.

The three lads knew that they would be shown into the counting and drug weighing room, down a corridor behind the front door. They rarely saw any other room.

This was the largest of all the rooms and was where the money was counted and sorted, and from which the drugs they dealt were packed and distributed.

There was no name to this enterprise. 'Names,' Warren once argued, 'are like fuckin' ID tags. They get you noticed by the authorities and other gangs, they get you known and targeted. Never, ever be linked to a named crew,' he had said forcefully. 'Fuckin' bad news.'

As was Warren Evan himself: fucking bad news. A man who could cause terror.

The security man – they didn't even know the guy's name – paused with his fist up at the door.

From behind came the dull thud of music.

The man beat on the door.

Then he looked at the three lads. His piss-coloured eyes went to each of them in turn, and back. He had an unspoken thought, then turned to face the door again and banged again.

There was a buzzing sound – the door release – and the door opened fractionally.

He pushed it and they filed in, the three of them glancing worriedly at each other.

The security man led them along the tight corridor and into the counting room at the end. The furniture in this big room was sparse. One long thin table – actually two pasting tables screwed together and reinforced – on which lay a pistol, stacks of bagged white powder, overflowing ashtrays and a cash counting machine presently flicking through a thick wad of twenty pound notes. Caleb was feeding it from a pile of notes. The distinctive aroma of weed combined with cigarette smoke hung in the air.

Warren lounged in a director's chair behind the table, slouched low, legs crossed, relaxed.

The security man peeled away and the three lads stood in front of Warren, rather like a group of naughty schoolboys being paraded on in front of a strict headmaster. A strict headmaster, though, had nothing on the two men behind that pasting table.

Leon swung the plastic bag he'd been carrying into a space on the table. It crashed down, clattering with the weight of gold inside, the takings from their last two armed robberies at Dalvinder's pawn shop and Cash4Gold. Caleb knew a scrap metal merchant who had an 'in' to the gold trade and gave good prices for the kind of stuff Caleb could get for him, which was melted down into rough ingots and then filtered into the legitimate gold business. Easy cash. Good for turnover. And no doubt some of it down the line would end up being traded into shops such as Cash4Gold. And then he might steal it back again. 'A circle of life thing, innit,' Caleb once boasted.

Caleb began sorting through the trinkets.

Warren, however, did not even glance at the pile.

Instead he was looking at Leon, Danny and Rob. From one to the other and back again. Curious, his brow furrowed.

Then he broke the very brittle silence.

'Where's my brother?'

***

There was no other way to describe it: Warren exploded.

He had to ask the question again. 'Where's my bother?'

He saw the exchange of apprehensive looks between Rob, Leon and Danny.

Caleb raised his head from his sorting task at that point, sensing something amiss. He placed down the gold ring he'd been inspecting.

Warren reached back and turned down the volume of the hi-fi; the drum-bass beat ricocheted around the room for a few seconds, then died. He raised his chin, eyeing the three guys, his gaze eventually coming to rest accusingly on Rob, the most senior.

He did not ask the question a third time.

Rob swallowed something heavy in his throat, then said sheepishly, 'He's dead, Waz.'

Warren blinked, took a second to absorb the news, confused by what he had just heard. He glanced at Caleb, whose face was in instant shock. For a moment, Warren seemed to be handling it well, though struggling to get his head around it.

So the news having been broken, and Warren apparently taking it so well, Danny felt confident to interject, 'Old prick was tooled up, man…'

But he – they – had completely misjudged Warren. If they'd had the time to think it through, this was not the way Warren handled any bad news. And before Danny had chance to finish his explanation, Warren flipped over the counting table, sending its contents crashing everywhere and he was at Rob's throat in that very explosion of rage.

Rob didn't even fight back.

Within an instant, Warren had smashed Rob up against the wall, his forearm jammed across his throat, crushing Rob's windpipe. Rob's eyes popped out and Warren's face was nose-to-nose with Rob's, his eyes wild, his reaction feral.

'You was meant to have his back,' he growled. He bounced Rob off the wall, then drove him back up against it, giving him a chance to utter, 'We'll get him, man, we'll get him … we found out where he lives.'

Warren kept him pinned to the wall, thinking, running the whole thing through his mind.

Caleb watched the assault without moving, but then he stepped forward and moved in close behind Warren's shoulder with a sinister, knowing air. Referring to the gold and everything else in the flat, he said, 'We don't need no one coming looking.' He paused a second, then said, 'Put him down.'

He wasn't talking about Rob.

***

They had driven home in a tense silence and Sandra had not pushed George to talk. He wasn't the greatest at the deep stuff and beyond their marriage and son, this was probably the deepest subject they had ever encountered.

George had killed someone.

That was the fact. The simplicity of it. And the complexity of it.

It had been in self-defence, of that there was no doubt. And it had been an accident, because George had never intended to kill.

But Sandra knew he would not open up about it until he was good and ready to do so, nor would she force him.

So they arrived home in silence. She prepared a quick meal which they sat and ate in front of the TV, Sandra glancing continually at George but seeing him trapped in his own thoughts, staring with lifeless eyes at the TV which was just white background noise, mechanically putting food into his mouth using a fork in his left hand and eating as though it tasted of cardboard.

Sandra was devastated, struggling to hold back her tears, her mouth quivering until she could finally eat nothing more. The two mouthfuls she had swallowed had gone down reluctantly at best.

Eventually she said, 'George, you know I'll be by your side, don't you, darling?'

He nodded and placed his tray down on the coffee table, inhaling a jagged breath. He opened his mouth to say something but no words came out as there was a loud knock on the front door.

Sandra gave a wilting sigh and glanced at the clock.

'I'll get it,' George said.

Sandra collected the trays while George stood up, went into the hallway to the front door and placed his left eye to the spyhole.

***

They moved along the road, silent, keeping to the shadows. As they entered the garden, Danny and Warren peeled off and ran down the side of the house to get to the back door. Rob and Leon went to the front.

Leon knocked, then flattened himself against the wall. In his hand he carried a sledgehammer.

Rob pulled out a long Phillips screwdriver and hammer from his coat, placed the cross-head tip of the screwdriver up to the spyhole in the door and rested the hammer on the butt-end of the screwdriver.

He waited.

He heard movement behind the door. Then George's voice. 'Who is it?'

Rob then struck the hammer hard against the screwdriver, smashing it through the spyhole and into George's eye, which was at that very moment up to it. He crashed back with a scream, blood spurting from a pierced eyeball.

Rob and Leon then forced their way through the door, using the sledgehammer and flat-footing it open. It clattered back on its hinges and the two lads were in – and on the doubled-up George. Rob took him and in one swift move grabbed George's hair, forced him back against the wall and suddenly there was a long bladed, military style knife in his hand which he held across George's mouth, corner to corner. This was the knife Rob had pointed at George before leaving the Cash4Gold shop – and he was now making good the gesture.

Leon stepped in behind, closing the front door after checking the street with a shifty glance and a satisfied smile. They had entered unseen and unheard.

Around the back of the house, Warren and Danny found that the door was unlocked. As soon as they heard the crash from the front, they were in, storming into the kitchen and confronting Sandra.

She'd heard the commotion at the front, placed the trays on the drainer and was rushing to investigate when the door burst open and Warren and Danny came at her.

She screamed, but Warren was on her, silencing her with a brick-hard punch to the side of the head, sending her crashing against a cupboard. Warren grabbed her before she fell and slung her face-down across the kitchen table, leaning his whole weight over her and twisting the point of a small knife into her cheek.

'You keep your mouth shut, cunt,' he whispered, his lips actually touching her ear, 'or I cut your fucking tongue out.'

Danny stepped in close and cocked his head to get a better view of Sandra's face and body.

Warren glanced at him. 'Fuck you doin'?' he demanded.

'She's a MILF, mate,' Danny said, a dreadful expression on his face.

Mother I'd Like To Fuck.

They exchanged a knowing glare, which Sandra read and understood. She started to struggle. 'No, no…'

Warren kept her easily pinned down by his weight, kept the knife to her face, and he jerked his free hand up her skirt, feeling for her cunt. She writhed, but Warren held her tight.

In the front hallway, Rob spat into George's face as he demanded, 'Put your fuckin' hands together.' Rob backed off slightly, but kept the knife blade held across George's mouth, and Leon moved in to tape George's wrists together, binding them tight with duct tape. As he did so, Rob's finely honed knife blade cut into George's skin and blood started to trickle down the side of his chin.

The sound of Sandra's screams came from the kitchen, terrifying George, who moaned desperately.

Rob came right up to his face again. Eyeball to eyeball 'Yeah,' he hissed, 'I'd be going fuckin' mental, wonderin' what's happenin' to my missus if I were you, mate…'

In the kitchen, Warren and Danny tore at Sandra's clothes, ripping off her skirt, tights and panties, exposing her, keeping her pinned down to the table, her face distorted. Warren began unzipping his jeans, feeling for his hard cock.

In the hall, George and Rob were still face to face, listening to the now muted screams, the crashing noises, the blade still in place across George's mouth.

Rob continued to taunt the powerless George, still whispering, his eyes blazing victoriously as he spoke. 'Think you had some bollocks earlier, did ya? Fuckin' hero? Hero, are ya?' he demanded. 'Bet when they let you out on bail you couldn't wait to tell the missus. "Here, babe, guess what I did today? Stopped some 'orrible fuckers from robbin' me shop. Killed one of 'em as well. What's for dinner?"'

George struggled to speak, to plead, to explain himself.

Rob was relentless. 'Problem is, mate, the lad you killed, yeah? His brother is in there with your missus right now.'

George emitted a moan of hopeless despair.

Rob smiled mock-sympathetically, like he was a mate. 'Come on, don't be like that. You need to lighten. Fella can't go through life without a grin once in a while – so why don't you give us a really big...' Rob sliced the knife across George's mouth, deep and hard. '...Smiley face?'

***

They were positioned, purposely, facing each other. Both now had pieces of duct tape over their mouths. Their arms and ankles were bound to chair arms and they looked at each other, somehow trying to convey love and hope.

Sandra was still naked from the waist down, blood running between her legs from the terrible assault she had endured.

George's punctured left eye bled, as did his mouth, which had been sliced horribly apart.

Warren looked at them for a moment before lifting the petrol can and starting to splash its contents over the couple.

The other three watched from the garage door, mesmerised by Warren and buzzing from what they had achieved: total revenge.

Warren allowed the final dribble of petrol to drop onto George's head.

To Leon, he said, 'Start the motor.'

Leon whined. 'Fuck that, I wanna see them go up, man.'

'You'll go up with them if you hang about here. Go on, fuck off with Danny and sort the motor.'

Reluctantly, they left.

Warren dropped the empty can, then leaned into George's terrified face. 'You're lucky, bruv. See, I didn't get to say goodbye to my brother when you smashed his brains in, but see, this way, at least you get to say goodbye to each other. I put a bit more petrol on her,' he added cruelly, 'so hopefully she'll go first.'

Warren patted George on the shoulder and ripped the tape off his mouth. He moved to the door that led back through to the house, smacking the punch bag that hung from the garage ceiling as he passed it, to where Rob stood. He stopped, turned back, took some cover behind the door and then lit a match which he flicked into the garage with a manic laugh. They both watched for a second, then quickly left, slamming the door behind them, hearing the 'whoosh' of flames as the fire turned the garage into an incinerator.

++++

FOUR

He came into the city under the cover of darkness, the plane touching down just before midnight. He made his way unopposed and unchallenged through immigration and customs, emerging at the taxi rank, climbing straight into a black cab. He gave the driver the address and sat back, deep in unsettling thought, absently rolling the gold wedding band on his finger. An unconscious habit. Suddenly he realised what he was doing and lifted his hand, angling it so the fluorescent street lights reflected off the metal. He stared at this for a long time, his mind churning.

Jimmy Vickers was a man returning home, but home to a place that, within the flash of a flame, had changed irrevocably.

***

The rain fell hard and the flowers hung limp and wet in Jimmy's hand. He stood there alone, head bowed, rain cascading off his close cropped hair, dripping off his nose.

Then he stooped and placed the flowers by the headstone which was already surrounded by dozens of bouquets and floral wreaths to the loving couple and parents whose charred bodies lay interred beneath that earth.

It was a simple headstone. At first glance, Jimmy had decided he would replace it with something more ornate, but standing there reading it, he started to think that its simplicity was its strength.

'IN LOVING MEMORY OF GEORGE VICKERS AND SANDRA VICKERS. "AND GOD SHALL WIPE AWAY ALL THE TEARS FROM THEIR EYES AND THERE SHALL BE NO MORE DEATH".'

***

He was alone in the underground carriage, the rhythm of the wheels on the tracks mirroring the beat of his heart.

He had earphones plugged into his mobile phone, the wires running up across his chest into his ears. He listened repeatedly to the voice messages.

His face constricted with grief as the sound of his mother's chirpy voice filtered into his brain.

'Hi Jimmy ... hope you get home okay and you enjoy your flight and it isn't too bumpy.' She sounded thrilled by the prospect of her only son's expected arrival home. Jimmy's lips twitched. She was always excited by him and he always shook his head in pretend despair at her, the fussing, the hugs, the kisses. Her son. She loved him, he loved her and although he knew he did return the love, now, sitting on that underground train as it clattered below London and plunged into a long, deep tunnel, he wished he had shown her his love more than he had done. Her light, tuneful voice went on, 'Know how much you hate flying ... so, anyway, I'm doing a big chicken on Sunday and...'

Not that he would have been home on the Sunday that she was referring to.

Events in the desert had seen to that.

In the background of the voice message, he heard his father call out, shouting over his mother.

Jimmy's fists bunched like rocks as he heard the deep timbre of that voice. He was the man Jimmy looked up to, the man who had always been there for him, no matter what crap Jimmy had thrown at him. Who had loved and supported and guided him; whose values of love, loyalty and honour Jimmy had admired, respected, and which had become Jimmy's own code of living.

'Tell him about the punch bag,' George Vickers had called over his mother's voice. And in those few words Jimmy picked up the happiness in his dad's voice – the fact that his son was returning from a grubby war halfway across the world.

His mother came back on. 'Ooh, yeah, your dad's cleaning out the garage and he wants to know if you want that old punch bag that's still hanging up, or can he throw it out? He'll keep it if you want it, but he's getting too old for it now.' She laughed.

***

Jimmy stood at the floor to ceiling window of his apartment, staring across the peerless cityscape that was London by night. Rain struck the window, hard, relentless. The view through the downpour made the city sparkle, and just visible in the distance was the top half of the London Eye, lit up in azure. Even from behind the window, Jimmy could feel the beat of the city.

He stood up to the reflection in the glass, taking in his own image, not sure what he was seeing or who he was any more.

At the one time in his life when he most needed the roots and strong foundation that were his parents, they had been taken violently away from him by violent men.

But Jimmy was also a violent man.

He took a long sip of his freshly made whiskey and Coke with ice as he watched his reflection. On a glass topped table next to him was his mobile phone, earplugs removed, loudspeaker on, replaying his mother's last message to him.

'...And anyway, give us a call whenever you get this, whenever you can ... whatever,' she said becoming flustered as her emotions started to grip her. 'You know what I mean. Can't wait to see you. Love you. Bye.'

Jimmy raised his glass to the city, to himself, to the memory of his parents.

The voice mail whirred on. 'Message six,' the metallic female voice informed him flatly. 'Received Friday, November seventeenth, at nine fifty-four pm.'

There was a slight pause.

Then came the sound of another familiar voice, echoing through the apartment.

Jimmy turned his head and looked at the phone. 'Jimmy?' the message started hesitantly. It was his old friend Tony Griffin. 'God, mate,' he said desperately. 'I don't know what to say. I'm so sorry. Listen, when you get back, give us a shout. We'll get 'em, mate, I promise you. I love ya, mate. Talk to you soon...' There was a long silence, then. 'End of messages.'

Jimmy sank the last of his drink, the ice clashing against his bared teeth. He moved away from the window, grabbed his jacket and phone.

Decision made.

***

He was a man who, if he chose, could walk unseen through a city or a desert or a jungle. That night it was a city. Through the streets of Piccadilly, hood up, hunched into his jacket, he moved unnoticed by the late night denizens of that part of London, many of them also loners of the metropolis, people far, far different from those of the day. Jimmy drifted through them like a phantom, people passing him then furrowing their brows for a moment, wondering if they had actually seen someone or was it just a figment of their imagination. Often they turned to look – and saw no one – but then they carried on, immersed in their own lives with maybe just a puzzled shrug of their shoulders.

But, like a shape changer, Jimmy Vickers could then morph into a different body when he wanted his presence to be felt. Just by use of body language, he could become very noticeable and make people give him a wide berth if that was the edge of him he wanted to portray, just as easily as he could disappear into a crowd or a desert.

As he stepped through the front door of The Wolf pub, his whole persona changed. He pushed through the inner doors and paused on the threshold to take in the bar beyond.

The Wolf. A regular haunt of his father's, premises in which he was well known. A usually bustling, stereotypical central London pub catering for locals, similar to a hundred others. Just a bar, hardly any space to move, quaint fixtures and fittings reminiscent of a bygone age, but nothing fancy. A place of character for the people.

For a moment, a hush descended as the regulars turned their heads and made eye contact with Jimmy.

He did not make eye contact with any of them, even though he did take in every familiar face. Chatter restarted as Jimmy – his presence now keenly felt – went to lean on the bar.

The barmaid came up to him apprehensively. Her name was Debbie. She knew Jimmy, knew his parents, knew what had happened. Her eyes tried to console him with sympathy.

'Hi Jimmy, how you feeling?' she asked quietly.

As Jimmy was about to answer, the landlord of The Wolf stepped in between them, easing Debbie gently aside to stand opposite Jimmy.

'It's alright Debs,' he said. To Jimmy, 'Alright Jimmy, how're you keeping?'

Terry Cole was trying to be friendly, but underneath his guts churned at Jimmy's appearance which had sent a shockwave around the bar. More than most, Terry was aware of what had happened to Jimmy's parents. And more than most, he knew of Jimmy's reputation and what their death might mean to him as an individual. Terry had just cause to be wary in the extreme.

Jimmy half nodded.

'Drink?' Terry asked.

'Can I get a Coke, please?'

'Yeah, yeah,' Terry said with relief. Maybe Jimmy had not come to mix it after all, but his aura said something different. Terry turned to the chiller cabinet at the back of the bar while Jimmy, leaning on his elbows, surveyed the room, noting that many of the punters were talking in hushed tones now, taking surreptitious glances in his direction.

No one wanted to eyeball him.

They just didn't.

Terry placed an ice filled glass on the bar, started to fill it with Coke from a bottle. He pushed the glass towards Jimmy.

There was an awkward silence – one engineered by Jimmy. He liked silences. People felt an obligation to fill them. That was when they incriminated themselves.

Like Terry.

'Look, I'm sorry about what happened,' he said.

Jimmy held Terry in a paralysing lethal look. 'I'm sure you can point me in the right direction, Tel.' He took a sip from the coke, eyeing Terry over the rim of the glass.

Terry's mouth clammed shut into a guilty line.

'Must've seen something,' Jimmy probed.

'I didn't see anything, Jimmy. It all happened in the middle of the night. No one heard nothing.'

Jimmy sipped the Coke, seeing that Terry was lying. His words were rushed and flustered. A man under pressure.

Jimmy stated evenly, 'You live fifty yards away.'

Terry held up the palms of his hands. 'I'm sorry Jimmy, I really am, but if you're here to cause trouble, maybe you should go, mate.'

Debbie had watched and listened to the exchange. She said, 'Terry,' in a way that said, 'Tell him, tell him what you know.'

Terry shot at her, 'Stay out of this.'

Jimmy watched this exchange, then asked, 'Trouble?'

He placed the Coke down on the bar top, slightly to one side so there was a clear space between him and Terry – just one of those tiny but important things that people like Terry didn't notice, but should have done.

There was no warning. Jimmy struck. He lunged across the bar, fast, hard, and grabbed the front of Terry's shirt, yanked him over and up close – and the Coke did go flying, as it happened. But he had Terry there, twisting his grip on Terry's shirt front, his eyes terrible to behold ... the phantom had become a demon.

Suddenly, one of the other customers stepped in misguidedly to help and grabbed Jimmy from behind, hauling him off Terry, who toppled backwards into the glasses shelves, then over.

Jimmy went with the momentum initially, then gave the man who had pulled him off Terry a reverse head butt, smashing the back of his skull into the man's unprotected face. He tore himself out of the man's grip, twisted on the spot with the grace of a ballet dancer and fired two accurate punches into the man's throat. He dropped like a stone, gurgling, blood gushing from his busted nose.

Jimmy spun again and vaulted easily over the bar top. He dropped light footed behind it on the balls of his feet, standing menacingly over Terry, who was struggling to get back up.

Debbie rushed forward, coming between the men.

'Jimmy, wait,' she pleaded, then jerked her head around to Terry, sitting numbly on his backside, gasping and frightened. 'Tell him, tell him for Christ's sake.'

'I called the fire service,' Terry admitted weakly, still on his arse.

On hearing the words, Jimmy came back down from the peak as he saw Terry crumble, tears forming in his eyes as he explained, 'I called the fire service...' His voice went flat as he recalled the night. 'There were four of 'em, they broke in ... I could hear your dad screaming and I watched.' He raised his eyes defiantly – but there was also defeat in them. 'I watched from the window because I was scared. OK?'

'Who were they?' Jimmy said coldly.

Terry shook his head slowly, dropped his eyes.

Jimmy turned, was gone.

***

Jimmy heaved up the garage shutter door, tearing off the criss-crossed crime scene tape which was still pinned from corner to corner, although the garage had been abandoned as a crime scene days ago.

He stood there for a moment, looking in.

This was going to be one of the toughest moments in his life. He would much rather have gone hand-to-hand with a ferocious Taliban fighter than do this. But if there was one thing Jimmy Vickers had, it was the courage to face anything.

He stepped into the garage, the stench of the fire invading his nostrils. And in that smell was the scent of burnt human flesh, something that Jimmy knew well. He had entered many buildings in Afghanistan in which the occupants had been burned alive.

He knew how it reeked.

He knew how they had screamed.

A dreadful death. One of the worst.

He paced slowly through the scorched remains of the interior, looking at everything, hypothesising, imagining … an overturned chair, burned black, almost cinders. Old shoe boxes, blackened shelves, the remains of a plastic Christmas tree. He stopped and looked at what was nothing more than a twisted metal pole in a triangular stand, nothing left of the branches. The Christmas tree that had been in the family since he was born. Getting a little more ragged every year, forcing his mother to wrap more tinsel around it to thicken out the sparse branches, add more baubles … it became a standing joke between the three of them but his mother, typically, would not relent and buy a new one. She had bought it for Jimmy's first Christmas and its memories had been powerful to her. Now, it had been destroyed.

Jimmy glanced at the garage ceiling. Water dripped continually from a burst pipe.

In the corner of the garage, somehow still hanging there, was the punch bag.

Dad's punch bag.

He stepped over to it, running his fingertips across its now charred leather outer coat.

The memories of this, too, were intense.

His dad, who could've been a pro, teaching young Jimmy how to throw and land a punch, the science of it all. The both of them dancing around the bag over twenty years ago, laughing breathlessly, then eventually falling into an exhausted embrace.

Great days, still very much with him.

Torn away.

He bent to look – and amazingly, he could still see lines of chalk drawn across the bag. Jimmy's age and height through the years until he was twelve – and by then he was far too tall to measure.

'Fuck,' he said.

At his feet was an old tin box, scarred by flame, but still intact, the contents preserved. Jimmy bent down and flipped off the lid, knowing what was inside.

Photographs.

The one on top was a six by four of him standing between his mum and dad in the garden. It was a sunny day, taken the year before. His father was laughing and Jimmy was planting a big wet kiss on his mum's cheek as she laughed, too. She had loved this picture and had several copies made of it.

And now, here, Jimmy Vickers cried.

***

'How you feelin'?'

Jimmy turned slowly. He had heard the approach and guessed who it was. Tony Griffin, a close friend from boyhood since they had met in a schoolyard at the age of six and grown up together before, as always happens, they went their separate ways. But they tried to stay connected, and when they met up it was as if there never had been any gap, just picking up where they left off – like all true friends are capable of doing. Jimmy folded the photograph of himself and his parents, one that Griff had actually taken, and slid it into his jacket with care.

He gave his friend – who was standing there in full police uniform, clearly on duty – a look that said, 'How would you feel?' in response to the question.

'You're not doing yourself any favours by beating the shit out of people for info,' Griff said, and Jimmy then knew that he had been called to The Wolf, probably by one of the panicky regulars, to investigate a disturbance. Terry wouldn't have had the bottle to call the cops.

'Somebody knows something,' Jimmy stated.

Griff sighed. Too many years of on the beat coppering had shown him the reality of what people saw and what people didn't see. 'Maybe they do,' he conceded, 'but doing this job for all these years, you realise it's every neighbour's God given right to turn a blind eye for fear of getting a knife through the belly. Stop poking around, Jimmy.'

It was as though he hadn't heard these words of wisdom. 'What've you got?' Jimmy asked bluntly.

Griff gave a contemptuous snort of derision and knew he would not get anywhere with Jimmy, obstinate bastard. 'Nothing. No one's talking. One of the neighbours said they heard some commotion about eleven, thought it was just TV. Fire brigade were called at eleven thirty-eight when they saw the garage go up in flames and what was thought to be a red Ford Focus speeding off.'

Jimmy stared at the floor as Griff spoke, his tears now gone.

Griff continued. 'There's been a few raids like the one on your old man's shop. We're sure it's the same crew. Whoever they are, Jimmy, they scare people. They're evil.'

But Jimmy's mind had suddenly transfixed itself onto a terrible thought. 'Were they alive?'

'Jimmy … mate … don't,' Griff implored.

Jimmy cut in sharply. 'I said, were they burnt alive?'

Griff swallowed, not wanting to answer. But he did. His nostrils dilated as he revealed, 'Post mortem suggests they burned to death, yes.'

Jimmy raised his face as he took this in. Griff watched him with concern.

'Have you slept since you got back?'

Again, Griff's words did not seem to register. 'Can you get me the CCTV footage from dad's shop?' He stepped toward Griff, who was now under real pressure. He was anxious to help his friend in any way he could, but snaffling evidence wasn't that simple and even if nothing came of it, it could land Griff in a whole heap of trouble. Something that could lose him his job.

'Jimmy, I've seen it mate. It's just tracksuits, hoodies and masks.'

Jimmy was only two feet from his friend now, looking deep into him, mate to mate. He didn't need to ask the question again as Griff's resolve collapsed.

'I'll bring it to you tomorrow.' But I don't know how I'll get it, he thought.

Jimmy gave a curt nod, walked past Griff out of the garage.

'Jimmy,' Griff called. Jimmy stopped, looked back. For a moment, the words stuck in Griff's throat. 'Stood his ground, you know. Your old man.'

Jimmy nodded, almost smiled. Then he turned and was gone.

***

Jimmy had decided that this was the last place he would visit and pay his respects. In some ways he didn't even know why he felt the need to visit the church, other than he wanted to be close to them one last time before it all started.

It was over two hundred years old with a high vaulted roof, and the central aisle between the pews led to an intimidating altar with a full-size figure of Jesus Christ on the cross, blood trickling from his hands and side and down his forehead from the crown of thorns.

Jimmy moved along the aisle, sitting down under the Lord's watchful eye on a front row pew.

He still wasn't sure why he was here. He wasn't religious. His dad hadn't been either, but his mother prayed regularly and attended services.

It was just … right for him to be there.

He sat in silence, pulled the folded photograph from his pocket and looked at it.

A figure emerged from the shadows, sat alongside him.

Jimmy's lips pursed as he folded the photo and slid it away again.

Then he turned to look at the woman.

His wife. His soon-to-be ex-wife.

She was just slightly younger than him, her hair tied back, dressed in jeans and a short jacket. Pretty – Jimmy thought she was the prettiest girl he had ever seen when he met her over ten years ago, as she bounced into a stupid party at Griff's with all her mates, most of whom were drunk out of their skulls. But not Morgan. She could have all the fun she wanted without alcohol, and her natural, bubbly self had lit up the room, seemed to isolate her in Jimmy's vision. He could not take his eyes off her and although things between them had deteriorated, the one thing she had retained was her beauty.

As Jimmy looked sideways at her, she still took his breath away.

But now, her natural ebullience was hidden by cautious reserve.

'Missed the funeral,' she said accusingly, but softly.

He gestured at the church. 'Trying to make up for it.'

'When did you get back?'

'Friday.'

'I emailed you four, five times, Jimmy. Texted you.'

'Combat mission. Helmand Province,' he said tightly.

Morgan's full lips twitched cynically. One thing she had not lost, either, was the ability to spot Jimmy's lies. To her, but to no one else, Jimmy Vickers was an open book. 'Your commanding officer said you'd been arrested and detained.'

Jimmy's face creased with the pain of being rumbled. He sat back against the hard pew and inhaled.

Morgan watched his profile, then spotted the wedding ring still on his finger.

'What happened?' she asked.

'Morgan, you know I can't tell you.'

Anger rushed through her and her voice rose an octave. 'I think you can tell me, Jimmy, especially when I had to arrange and cover for you at your own parents' funeral.' She glared at him, lips set rigid, then the anger dissipated as suddenly as it came. She pulled herself together and her words echoed away.

Jimmy bounced forward and got up, moved past her to leave.

'Wait,' Morgan blurted.

He stopped. Morgan spoke more softly now. 'I'm sorry … just … look, you don't have to be on your own. Come by the house, you know?'

Jimmy took this in and nodded before striding down the aisle towards the church doors. Morgan turned around in the pew, watching him go all the way.

++++

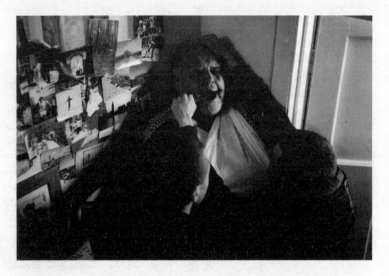

George Vickers (Tony Denham) is savagely attacked by the gang in a terrifying home invasion

Jimmy Vickers (Danny Dyer) pays a visit to his parents' graves

FIVE

Warren razor-bladed the coke into fine lines on the glass-topped coffee table, snorting it up ferociously through a rolled up fifty pound note, as though by doing so it would hit him harder and deeper and maybe take away some of the edge of his anger, which, even he knew, needed to be curbed. He was the ultra-violent boss, of that there was no doubt, and what he said was the word and the law, and he ruled everything with violence and intimidation as a matter of course, but the past couple of weeks, since Josh's death and the retribution meted out as a consequence, had been a hard time for him. He had tried to come down, to cool it all, but it was a problem.

And everyone was treading very carefully around him, terrified in case they did or said anything to upset him and tilt his grief into violence yet again.

But today had been pretty cool.

Maybe the first day of a return to normality for the gang.

A day spent chillaxing at Warren's house – not up in the tower block fortress – listening to music, drinking and snorting good quality cocaine and consuming delivered takeaways.

A great day.

Warren tipped his head back and flopped on the old settee.

Leon and Rob knelt by the coffee table, tapping out their lines of coke, getting an almost professional pleasure in keeping them completely straight.

Danny appeared at the living room door, escorting a young couple behind him. Instantly, everyone became tense: interlopers, strangers, were unwelcome in this environment – and in particular this geeky looking couple who seemed very, very out of place and nervous.

Warren demanded, 'Who the fuck is this?'

Danny could see he had made a mistake but kept it bright. 'This is Ryan. He's alright, Waz, just wants some gear.'

They were very definitely out of place.

Ryan, hair gelled, side parting, light blue polo shirt buttoned right up to the neck; Cassie, blonde with a very obvious spray tan and a tight, short top over large, freely swinging breasts.

Ryan babbled enthusiastically – and uneasily, 'Heard your stuff's awesome.' He reminded Warren of a politician in the making, a fucking hooray Henry twat.

'Get them the fuck out of here,' Warren said dismissively to Danny. 'Bring 'em to the flat in business hours.'

'Waz – they want half an ounce!'

'We're havin' a party,' Ryan said, sowing a seed. Rob glanced at Warren and it clicked.

***

They led the couple through to the garage where Warren carefully weighed off half an ounce of coke into a clear plastic bag, then took it off the scales. He eyed Ryan malevolently. 'Let's see the readies then, fella.'

Ryan pulled a folded wad of notes from his back pocket. 'How much?' he inquired, just checking.

'Five.'

'Five? Your guy told us four.'

'Five,' Warren affirmed.

'We've only got four on us,' Ryan sighed and looked at Cassie.

She said to Ryan, 'Just get four hundred's worth.' She was deeply unhappy with the situation, now surrounded by four jumpy, dangerous individuals, the air of menace tangible. She didn't like it, wanted to get out.

'I told 'em I'd get half an ounce,' he whined.

Warren cut in. 'Tell you what.' His eyes flickered conspiratorially across each of his gang members, then came back to Ryan. 'Four hundred and your bird shows me her tits.'

'Just let us have four hundred's worth, mate.'

Warren pouted, shook his head, and the atmosphere took on an even more sinister turn. Danny, Rob and Leon grinned. They were uncertain about exactly what was going to happen, but were up for anything to follow Warren, who said, 'No deal, fella. Five hundred's worth and your bird's tits. A fuckin' bargain.'

'Let's just go,' Cassie said, the feeling in her stomach now one of terror. She was starting to experience Warren Evans's stock in trade.

Ryan – nervous, but strangely oblivious to his girlfriend's feelings – said, 'Babe, we need this gear.' He almost added, 'Get 'em out, let's get it sorted.'

Warren suddenly turned on a bit of charm, trying to sound reasonable. 'C'mon,' he cooed, 'it's only a flash. You ain't even wearing a bra are ya, you cheeky thing?'

It worked and Cassie even smiled. Maybe things wouldn't be so bad after all. She reached for the hem of her top, rolled it up and obliged Warren by flashing her huge breasts – just for an instant. She quickly rolled her top back down and gave him a 'there' look.

But a cloud of lust passed over Warren's face. He felt himself harden at the sight.

Ryan, now wanting to retreat, handed Warren the money and his hand snaked out for the bag of drugs.

'Hang on,' Warren said, flipping his thumb contemptuously through the notes. 'You honestly think I'd give you a hundred quid's worth of gear for just a look at her tits? Just a look?'

'Right, we're going,' Ryan said, trying to assert some authority. But his voice was a weak squeal, betraying his nerves. 'Give us our money back.' He held out his hand.

Warren held his gaze and pocketed the cash and for the first time properly, Ryan realised this was not going to end well.

'You ain't going anywhere, mate.'

Ryan spun as he heard the door shut. Danny had closed it and now leant nonchalantly against it, grinning as he pulled a small pistol from his waistband and held it casually by his leg. An unsubtle warning. Leon stepped up behind Ryan, who flashed another look at Warren: trapped.

Warren moved closer to Cassie but as he spoke to her, his eyes were firmly on Ryan, challenging. 'You get your gear after she's sucked my cock.'

In a panic, Ryan twisted, tried to flee. Leon grabbed him and slammed him down onto the garage floor, trapping him up against the wall. He kicked him hard, guts, face, flat-footing the side of his head, which smacked hollowly on the concrete floor, split his scalp. Ryan groaned and tried to fold himself into a protective foetal position, his hands covering his head, but was ultimately useless as Rob joined in the assault too. He ran at Ryan and booted his face like a rugby ball, feeling a satisfying crack of the gristle and bone that were Ryan's septum and cheekbone.

Cassie was transfixed in a horrified way – like a member of the public at a road traffic accident. Then she tried to stare down Warren. She was much, much braver than Ryan.

'What's it gonna be, babe?' Warren growled. 'They'll stop kicking when you start sucking.'

Realising that she had truly stepped into the worst kind of nightmare, she reluctantly peeled off her top, her breath juddering uncertainly.

Danny cheered from the door as Warren guided Cassie back to a nearby armchair, one with its stuffing bursting out, saying, ''Ere, let him be guys. She's up for it. Just hold him.'

Warren sat down and Cassie knelt between his legs, both of them going to unfasten his trousers and pull down his boxers to reveal a hard, erect cock. Cassie eased back the foreskin, making Warren gasp. He laid his head back, a groan stuck in his throat, as Cassie eased his prick away from his body and put her lips over the tip of it, then slid her hot mouth down the long, thick shaft.

Rob, witnessing this, uttered, 'This is awesome.' He fished out his mobile phone and moved alongside, starting to video the event. He knew Warren would like to see it all again.

Cassie eyed Rob distastefully and pulled away from the task. Warren jerked forward, angry. 'Don't fuck about bitch. Do it right or you ain't getting' nothin' and I'll throw you through the window.'

She took him back in her mouth, one hand cupping his balls, the other his shaft, and began moving slowly, rhythmically. Rob continued to film as Warren said, 'That's good girl,' and lay back his head again.

In the corner of the garage, a bloodied Ryan started to struggle, but Leon lay into him again, pounding his face to a pulp in time with the bobbing movement of Cassie's head.

***

'Now, he was a mess,' PC Jenny Clarke said to Griff as they left the A&E department and climbed into the police patrol car. 'And his girlfriend wasn't much help.'

'I agree with both statements,' Griff said, firing up the Vauxhall Astra.

'What d'you reckon then?' Clarke asked. 'He doesn't seem very keen to make a complaint, either. We're only here because the hospital called us – and the fact that the poor lad's going to need reconstructive facial surgery.'

'We need to rattle some cages at the very least,' Griff said, though he knew from experience they would hit a brick wall with this one. 'Let's knock on a door or two.'

'I'm up for that,' Clarke said.

Griff drove on and an unusual silence descended on the pair of them. Unusual because they were mostly a very talkative duo and got along quite well. Clarke squinted at him.

'Look,' she said, 'hope you don't mind me asking, Griff...'

'Uh, what?'

'Everything okay? You seem really distant at the moment, like something big's going on in that noggin of yours.'

'I'm okay ... honest.'

She could tell he was lying.

***

Half dressed, wearing only his jogging bottoms which were pulled up only half-way up his backside and only just covered his genitals, Warren lounged indolently on the door jamb and sneered at the two cops who had dared to knock on his front door. He felt no trepidation, no concern. He believed himself to be untouchable and above the law. He looked them both up and down with disrespect. Two woodentops and already he was planning on baiting them, winding them up – especially the female one. His eyes lingered dirtily on her.

'Fuck d'you want?' he demanded.

Griff said, 'We've had reports of a disturbance at this address a few hours ago.'

Warren's face remained impassive. 'So what?'

'Mr Evans – have you been at home all night?'

'Yeah.'

Clarke intercut, already feeling herself being wound up by this overconfident, rude individual. 'We have reason to believe a man was assaulted on your premises, a Mr Ryan Scott.'

'Don't ring any bells,' Warren smirked.

'Can we come in and chat?' Griff asked.

There was a beat while Warren composed himself for his response, which was, 'Fuck off.'

Then all three had a brittle moment of stand-off.

Warren grinning, cocky and in control. He lit up a cigarette and as he took his initial drag of it, dipped his right hand down the front of his joggers and scratched his testicles, eyeing Clarke as he did so, posturing and trying to provoke them.

Wearily, Griff said, 'There's a young man in hospital who's been badly beaten up. His face is a mess.' He stared at Warren, weighing the whole scenario up, knowing he could push it and heave Warren into the nick if he wanted – because there was always that power – but it needed to be balanced with the end result, which in this case might be nothing.

Warren's eyes hooded over. 'Listen pig, ain't nothin' to do with me, so take,' – he shook his cigarette at Clarke – 'this little fuck puppet here and fuck off outta my space.'

Griff almost rose to it. But he held back. He knew how to bide his time, and in this case the time would come when – or if – Ryan Scott made a statement, and not before. Without something written down, this would all come to nothing and Warren would probably sue the shit out of the cops just for fun. It was over a grand an hour pay-out for time spent in custody for an unlawful arrest. Griff had the feeling that Warren's solicitor would be all over the cops like a very bad rash.

Next to him, he could sense Clarke's tension at the insult and he didn't want her launching into something that might backfire. Griff turned, touched Clarke's arm and they walked away down the garden path.

But Warren couldn't just let it go – and did the thing that probably cost him his life.

He called after them, 'Don't you be a stranger, though, sweetheart. You pop back here any time you like.'

This stopped Clarke in her tracks, instantly furious. She spun. 'What was that?'

'You heard, babe.'

She stormed back up the path, Griff unable to stop her, and went nose-to-nose with Warren. 'In what reality do you honestly think I would be interested in a chavvy sack of shit like you?'

Warren screamed with laughter, lapping up this reaction. Just what he had been needling for.

Griff grabbed her arm. 'Whoa, whoa,' he said and pulled her away down the garden.

'Go on girl,' Warren shouted. 'That's it, Chief Wiggum, rein her in man. Gotta keep that little Pit Bull bitch on a leash.'

On the pavement, Clarke tore herself free from Griff's grip.

'Oi,' he said, trying to bring her back to earth. 'You cannot let them get to you.' But his words sailed over her head. She stormed off towards the police car.

Griff made to go after her, but something made him pause, mid-step. If Warren hadn't shouted the insult and if Clarke hadn't lost her cool, Griff might not have stopped to notice, but he did.

The car parked by the kerb outside Warren's house.

A red Ford Focus.

Griff looked at it, then back at the house, then his bottom lip drooped open and he took out his pen and a scrap of paper.

***

Jimmy Vickers was alone now, sitting in a café in central London, eating an all-day breakfast, sipping from a mug of tea. A good meal, capable of setting anyone up for anything.

He was in deep thought, still working through his grief and plans, his mind in turmoil. At the same time, he was very aware of his surroundings, the people around him, moving through this environment. The oldish couple sitting at a table nearby, engrossed in their food and the newspapers ... their usual routine, Jimmy guessed. The woman in her thirties sat hunched over a latte, continually texting, checking for messages on her mobile. Dealing with a relationship break-up, Jimmy thought.

Then the black man at the table in the corner of the café, neat but casually dressed. For less than a nanosecond Jimmy's eyes locked onto his, but the man went coolly with the flow of being clocked and dropped his gaze back to the magazine he was purporting to read.

Out of place.

Jimmy smiled inwardly, glanced across the street. The man on the corner, talking into his phone ... a very long conversation – not ... taking the odd sly look across at the café.

Out of place.

Jimmy felt a surge of excitement.

His own phone vibrated as a call came in. He snapped it up.

***

He knew he hadn't been followed because he'd gone through some basic anti-surveillance tactics of doubling around roundabouts, parking up, waiting, retracing steps, and simply watching. He couldn't have done anything fancy because he didn't have time, but he was as sure as he could be that he'd either shaken a tail or there wasn't one there to begin with.

When he pulled onto the piece of derelict ground by the Thames in east London, he knew he was alone.

It was still raining, battering down noisily on the roof of his Toyota Hi-Lux, the wipers having to trudge hard to clear the screen.

The passenger door opened and Griff slid in, handing Jimmy a USB stick.

'Owner of the red Ford Focus is one Warren Evans. It ain't registered to him, but he owns it, drives it, uses it. Three-three Hillside Avenue.'

'Sure it's them?'

'Warren Evans had a younger brother, Joshua.'

Jimmy snapped a look at Griff, the name instantly meaning something. 'Had?'

Griff continued, 'Joshua Evans was accidentally killed during an attempted robbery over two weeks ago after receiving a blow to the head from the shop keeper who was defending himself.' Griff paused. 'Your old man.'

++++

SIX

He was feeling good. Blood throbbed through his veins as he lifted the weights and then placed them on the rack for the last time. He sat up on the power bench, revelling in the feel of the sweat pouring off him, glancing down proudly at his toned, well-muscled body and arms, the result of tough workouts and supplements, legal and illegal. It was necessary to keep this fit and strong. There were times when his authority had to be asserted, and muscle power, combined with attitude – and the pleasure he got from hurting people – was the way in which Warren Evans did it.

Veins coiled around his biceps like steel cords.

He had once strangled someone by curling his arm around their throat. That had been a pleasing moment in his life – watching the young man turn blue, his eyes bulge bloodily out of their sockets, and finally the tongue lolling like a dead dog. He recalled it with fondness as he tensed his muscles, drawing an admiring glance from the two leotard-clad women walking across the gym floor, both sweating sexily from their Zumba workout.

Warren gave them his best boyish grin, utterly charming.

Life was fucking good.

Money, power, business and a choice of women.

Nice.

He stood up and walked into the men's changing rooms.

***

Warren was the last customer to leave the gym that night and the car park was virtually deserted. He walked with bounce, swagger and roll, reaching the Ford Focus and tossing his kit bag across the passenger seat before slotting in behind the wheel.

He didn't like the car, but it was a necessity in his line of business. Unremarkable and serviceable, a car people saw but easily forgot.

One day, he promised himself, in the not too distant future, he would buy himself something special when he had amassed enough cash to retire from the business. It was the dream of all crims, from Mafia bosses downwards: to go legit. That was the eventual aim, anyway.

Warren was no different. One day it would happen. As he inserted the ignition key and started the unwilling engine, this was his ambition.

What he did not know was that before this night was out, he would be dead.

***

Jimmy's car sat deep in the shadows in the unlit section of the car park. He had waited patiently – as he had been trained to do, as he had done on many occasions – ever since Warren had entered the gym two hours earlier and now he had emerged, fit for anything.

Jimmy liked the irony.

He watched Warren get into the Ford, saw the brake lights come on. He slammed the Hi-Lux into gear and accelerated across the unmade gravel surface of the car park, flicking up chippings like sparks, and rammed the back end of the Ford using the chrome steel bull bars fitted on the front of the Toyota. Warren's car shunted forward, stalled.

Jimmy sat unmoving, waiting for Warren's next move.

He was out in a flash, storming back towards Jimmy, staring wildly through the driver's door window but slightly nonplussed by the guy sitting in the car, refusing to make eye contact with him after having just rammed his car up the backside of the Focus.

Warren leaned into the already opened window, snarling, 'Fuck you doin', prick?'

Jimmy did not respond – something which, again, puzzled Warren, who reared back, looking at the car and its occupant, unable to figure any of this out.

'You gotta problem, mate?'

Again, no response. Which, of course, served to wind him up even more.

Warren reached into his pocket, pulled out a flick knife which he clicked open, ensuring it was in Jimmy's line of sight.

Now there was a reaction.

Slowly, Jimmy's head turned and his eyes met Warren's ... the look of the devil.

'Now you listen to me, you cunt,' Warren said, shaken by the look in a way he would never have thought possible.

Neither did he get chance to finish his sentence. Suddenly, Jimmy snapped open the car door, smashing it into Warren's body, knocking him backwards, the knife dropping from his grip.

Jimmy slid out of the car, his movements measured, deceptively slow.

Warren recovered, scooped up the knife and lunged at Jimmy. He moved quick, swiping horizontally across Jimmy's torso once, then slashing back and catching Jimmy's side, the blade slicing his stomach.

Jimmy caught Warren's wrist, twisting it back agonisingly and forced him to release the knife.

But Warren was very strong and he powered into Jimmy, punching repeatedly.

Jimmy rolled with the blows, ducking, weaving, returning a punch to Warren's face. He hit hard, but it had little effect and just seemed to galvanise Warren into an even more ferocious attack, and the encounter descended into a disjointed street fight for a few moments, blows delivered, glancing off, untidy, messy ... a scrap. But then Jimmy had had enough.

With a superbly aimed thrust kick, the edge of Jimmy's right foot connected with Warren's knee cap, dislodging it. He sagged down and Jimmy moved in, his head punches now hard, efficient and effective, one after the other, and Warren went down, unconscious.

Breathing heavily and injured, Jimmy stood over Warren's body.

***

It was the splashing sound of the liquid that permeated Warren's blackness. He came to groggily, his head pounding, disorientated. His blood-caked eyes opened and his senses started to filter back as he realised he was sitting in the driver's seat of his Focus, his wrists bound to the steering wheel with plastic cable ties. He tried to move his head and then knew it was duct taped securely to the headrest behind him and that the lower half of his legs had also been taped to the car seat, making all movement virtually impossible. From the vicinity of his right knee, came bolts of incredible pain. The busted joint had swollen to the size of a small melon.

A dark figure stood directly in front of him at the car's radiator grille.

Warren's eyes focused to watch this man as he moved around the car, splashing liquid all over it from a can.

Shit.

Petrol.

Warren squirmed, yanking at the wrist ties, and trying to free his head by using his powerful neck muscles, but he had been well secured. 'Are you fuckin' mental? What the fuck you doin?'

Jimmy dropped the can by the side of the car, then pulled on a pair of thin, black leather gloves. He lit a cigarette, placed it between his teeth.

Saying nothing, telegraphing nothing, he leaned in and punched Warren on the side of his head, three hard, disabling punches with his right fist into Warren's temple and cheek, smashing the cheekbone underneath Warren's right eye, bloodying his nose and cutting the inside of his mouth as the soft flesh connected with his teeth.

Warren swallowed hard, almost choking on his blood.

'Do you fucking know who I am?' Warren demanded. Then put a sneer into his voice. 'Big man, ain't ya? Beatin' a man with his hands tied. Cut me outta here and we'll see how long you last with me, you little dickhead.' He seemed to have forgotten that is exactly what had just happened – and he'd lost the battle.

Jimmy leaned in close. In his hand he had Warren's knife, the blood still on it from the cut in Jimmy's side.

Jimmy's voice did not rise. It was almost at conversational level. He spoke with the cigarette clasped between his teeth.

'I'm gonna ask you once. If I have to ask you twice, I'm gonna cut off your right ear. If I have to ask again, it's your left ear ... then it's your big, manly bollocks and cock.' He tapped the blade against Warren's ear and in time with each tap, he said, 'Does ... that ... make ... sense?'

Warren was now silent, his eyes turned to the corner of their sockets, watching the blade. For once, someone else was in charge and a shudder of helplessness went through him.

Warren Evans knew he was in very deep shit and could not control any of it.

Jimmy went on, still conversational. 'The couple…in the garage…a few weeks' back.'

Warren digested the words and his face registered his knowledge and guilt.

It was the answer Jimmy needed. The confirmation that he was on the right track.

And Warren realised it, too. He began to struggle desperately to free his hands and head and legs, terror being something he had only ever meted out to others, not something he had ever experienced himself, and it was a new – and fucking unpleasant – sensation to know that he had met someone more powerful, more evil maybe, and more cunning than himself.

He knew he was about to die.

Jimmy stepped back, standing casually. He took a drag of the cigarette – though he didn't inhale, because he didn't actually smoke.

But Warren, terrified though he was for the first time in his life, could not shake off the man that he was.

'You know what? Fuck you, mate. That prick killed my brother. Deserved what we did to him. You should've seen what we did to his missus.'

Jimmy's face did not change, although a new fire of rage started to burn within him. He controlled it, watching Warren, taking in the words.

And knowing he was going to die, that he had nothing left to lose, Warren decided to go out with a bang. He smiled, an expression contorted by his broken face. 'I'll bet you're their son or something, ain't ya? Mate, your mum's arse was so tight … niiiice, bruv.' He grimaced. 'We made 'em face each other, just before we fired 'em up. So they could watch each other burn. Fuckin' priceless,' he said and spat out a gob of blood that trickled obscenely down his chin.

Jimmy smiled, allowing he words to waft over him, content in the reaction that he was getting from Warren: fear.

'Listen,' Jimmy said. 'For being so honest, I'm gonna let you go – but you gotta do something for me first.'

'You're lying.'

'I ain't, mate.'

Jimmy leaned into the car again, his eyes close to Warren's – who was desperate to believe this, to clutch at any straw in spite of his bravado, wanting to be anywhere but here.

'Really?'

Jimmy nodded. 'I need the names of the others.'

'Nah.' Warren would have shaken his head if he could have moved it. 'Can't do it, man.'

'They'll never know,' Jimmy urged him softly, playing him, knowing that men in circumstances like this would often do anything if hope was dangled in front of them. And Jimmy had played many men before, most of them much more dangerous adversaries than Warren, who was nothing more than a jumped up street kid. Men who would give their lives for a cause, who saw death as something glorious … but also often wanted to live. Not always, but sometimes, and hope was a powerful weapon. Jimmy went on, 'It's black and white. You give 'em up, you live. You don't … well, you know the answer to that one.'

Warren was right on the knife edge. He wanted to believe this.

Jimmy encouraged him with a nod and raised eyebrows. 'Yeah?'

Warren nodded. Jimmy pulled a note book and pen from a pocket and leaned into the car, placed the book in one of Warren's hands, the pen in the other. There was just enough play in the way that Jimmy had tied the wrists so Warren could manoeuvre and write down the names. It was struggle, but he did it.

Warren thought he was a free man and his voice became calmer now, his confidence returning.

'Listen man, I'm well sorry 'bout what I just said then. Was bang out of order, just fucking lies, you know? Macho shit. Bet you think I'm a proper dickhead.'

Jimmy eased the notepad out of his fingers and studied the names as he drew on the cigarette. Warren eyed him hopefully, waiting for a response. Jimmy then glared at him, cold as frozen steel. He squatted down on his haunches by the car window. 'Can you imagine,' he began, and a tremor that he could not control came to his voice, 'what that must've felt like? Burning to death?' The rage was back in him now.

He stood up and lifted the petrol can and started to walk away from the car. Warren was bewildered – then it really hit.

'Hang on, hang on mate. You said you was gonna let me go.'

Jimmy kept walking slowly, allowing petrol to dribble out of the can, leaving a trail behind that shimmered.

Warren yanked at his wrists, squirmed, his whole body arching in his seat, trying to break free, crying desperately, 'Please mate. Oi! Bruv! Come back man. I'm sorry, I'm sorry, alright? Pleeease.'

Fifty metres from the car, Jimmy stopped, turned, pulled a long final drag on the cigarette so that its tip glowed red. Then he flicked it into the petrol trail.

It lit instantly with a whoosh. The fire slithered towards the doused car, then seemed to disappear underneath it.

Then nothing.

Jimmy waited. He knew it would happen. He had engineered it.

Then it went and the car burst into yellow and blue flames, the whump of the explosion raging over Warren's screams.

Jimmy watched for a long moment, the reflection of the fire flickering in his eyes. Then he turned and walked away, not flinching as a second explosion ripped the car apart with an ear-shattering boom.

He kept walking, his figure silhouetted against the flames.

++++

Jimmy (Danny Dyer) waits to ambush Warren

Jimmy (Danny Dyer) soon gets the upper hand in his battle with
Warren (Joshue Osei)

SEVEN

Afterwards, he drove for a long time. He could not pretend he hadn't been affected by what he'd done. To take any man's life was no easy decision, except for psychotic animals like Warren Evans to whom the life of another human being meant nothing – demonstrated in the lack of grief for his brother, Josh, and the thirst for revenge which he thought was a proper reaction to it. And, of course, in the cold blooded way he had wreaked that revenge.

Jimmy agonised over whether this was also a reflection of himself: grief leading to retribution and death.

'Am I any fucking better?' he demanded of himself.

As he swerved into the side of the road, he found himself breathless.

He pulled his left hand from the steering wheel and saw it was shaking and he had to clench his fist to stop it.

He held it up in front of his eyes, looking at it, then spread his fingers wide, his wedding ring glinting under the street lights.

***

The mug was hot. Jimmy wrapped his hands around it, comforted by the heat – as had happened on many occasions in Afghanistan, when returning from missions, a mug of hot tea was just as welcome as a pint of lager. He took a sip. It tasted good, warming his chest.

Of course in the desert, there would be the debrief, official and unofficial.

That would not be happening here tonight. Tonight, it would all be bottled up within himself.

He was in Morgan's big kitchen, sitting at the table next to the patio doors, overlooking the small, but perfectly formed rear garden of which Morgan was intensely proud.

She brought her mug and sat down opposite, pulling her house coat tight around herself. She pushed her mussed up hair back from her eyes and looked knowingly at Jimmy.

'Not sleeping, are you?'

He shook his head, stared into the mug at the tea which was the colour of bronze.

'Caffeine not a good idea, then?'

'Sun'll be up soon.'

Both looked automatically through the patio doors and the eastern sky was starting to lighten gradually as dawn tried to break through the November day.

'How have you been, anyway?' Jimmy asked her.

She nodded, pouted. 'Yeah, not bad. They moved the vets … bigger building, nicer … still studying finance.' She paused, blinking, her turn to look down at her tea, then, 'I'm really sorry for what happened.' Jimmy acknowledged this with a slight dip of his head and pained smile. 'You think it was retaliation for what your dad did?'

Another nod – but this time Morgan saw something behind Jimmy's expression which made her stomach tighten. That ability to read Jimmy who, to anyone else, maybe with the exception of Griff or Colonel Leach, was an impregnable, steel-plated shutter.

It was as if Morgan had X-ray vision into his soul.

'Promise me you won't do anything silly,' she said.

Jimmy didn't come back at her. 'Can I use your bathroom?' he asked, instead.

'Course.'

He took another warming sip of tea, then stood up. His coat flapped open to reveal his T-shirt underneath and the blood that had seeped into the material from the knife-slash wound.

Morgan saw it. 'What happened there?'

'Nothing.' Jimmy tried to cover it, but Morgan was up in front of him, holding his coat open.

'You're bleeding.'

'It's nothing,' he insisted weakly.

'Jesus, Jimmy. Sit down, take your coat off,' she insisted back – and her insistence won.

Like a reluctant child, he did as he was told, taking off his jacket and slinging it over a chair back. Morgan made him turn to face her and she bent down in front of him and delicately raised the hem of his T-shirt to reveal the wound which lay open, the blood coagulating around it. It wasn't a deep cut, but it needed to be treated, cleaned properly and stitched.

***

Jimmy sat back, arching his bare torso so that Morgan could easily deal with the wound. She pulled up a chair and sat in front of Jimmy. She swabbed the cut with an antiseptic wipe, then squeezed a line of cream onto it before starting to stitch it together.

Jimmy winced as the fine needle was inserted.

Their voices were soft as Morgan carried out this incredibly intimate procedure, her face close up to Jimmy's body as she worked, and Jimmy could feel her hot breath on his skin, almost feel the beat of her heart. He watched her concentrating on the task, the pulse throbbing in her neck, her skin so smooth and unblemished, her lips wide and full. She was the only woman he had kissed for a long, long time. He even once recalled telling her, during the lust of early courtship, that she had lips that needed to be kissed every day, many times a day – by him. He wondered why he had allowed it all to go so wrong,

'What happened?' she asked.

'Just some lads at the pub,' he answered, thinking she was referring to the cut. 'Me just being an arse.'

'In Afghanistan,' she corrected him.

Jimmy went tight lipped, brought down the veil. She glanced up, her eyes sparkling, then she grinned wickedly and pricked him with the needle.

'Alright, alright,' he submitted.

'I can think of worse way of getting you to talk.'

He composed his thoughts. 'It's complicated out there.'

She gave him a wry grin. 'Someone once told me that complication is a problem derived from the person, not the situation.'

Jimmy raised his eyebrows. 'Who? Was that me? I must've been pissed. I'm no philosopher.'

Morgan sniggered. 'Clown, more like.'

The silence between them returned as Morgan began to stitch. Jimmy glanced around and saw something on a chair nearby. He stiffened. Morgan sensed the change, glanced up and followed his line of sight.

A large brown envelope, on top of which was fanned out a sheaf of official looking, County Court letter headed papers that Jimmy recognised; after all, he had a copies of them, too.

Divorce papers. James Vickers v Morgan Vickers (nee Maxwell).

'I'll get round to signing those,' he promised.

'No rush,' she whispered.

Jimmy swallowed. 'Yeah, yeah, of course.' Suddenly a very dithery feeling jittered through him – the fear of losing the only woman he had ever loved in his life hit him like a sledgehammer. But he stayed composed. It was what she wanted and he understood. He would not be contesting anything.

Morgan finished the repair and snapped off the thread. 'Done,' she said with finality.

Jimmy looked down at the neat line. She moved away and glimpsed his back, an area covered in silvery burn marks, bullet weals and raised, ugly-looking scars, all of which told the story of Jimmy Vickers. A man who had seen the dark side of many battle fields and – incredibly – come out the other end, more or less in one piece. Morgan blinked back a tear.

Jimmy reached for his T-shirt.

'Wait – I need to put a dressing on it.' She took some white gauze from a first aid kit and taped it over the stitches. 'I usually do cats and dogs, but it'll do.'

'Thank you.'

'Pleasure.' She smiled reservedly and Jimmy eased himself painfully back into his T-shirt and jacket. 'It'll be a good scar. Hope you like 'em.'

'Used to 'em. How's yours looking?'

Morgan stuck out her left hand, revealing a white, five inch scar running across the base of her thumb onto the back of her hand and wrist.

'I saved your life that day,' Jimmy said, taking her hand with his left hand and inspecting the old wound, blinking at the memory.

'Pur-leese, I was hardly going to bleed to death.'

'Hey – we were twenty miles from a hospital in the middle of the Brecon Beacons,' he said, remembering her tumble. 'Anything could have happened.'

He rotated her hand and saw the pale band on her ring finger where her wedding and engagement rings had been. Morgan saw he was still wearing his.

Jimmy quickly let go and gestured he was about to leave.

'Thank you,' he said, 'for the tea and the surgery,' but both of them knew it was thanks for much, much more than that. He went out, Morgan watching him. He had reached the 4x4, was just about to climb in – determined not to look back over his shoulder, force himself to leave and never return, despite the beating of his heart.

In her bare feet, Morgan came up silently behind him. He spun and then she was in his arms, kissing him hard.

Within moments they were back in the house, then in her bedroom, kissing, devouring each other greedily, their clothing thrown aside. Then they were on the bed and the kissing became more thoughtful and less rushed as she moved under him, and Jimmy was deep inside her, knowing that he had arrived home.

++++

EIGHT

Not entirely sure where she and Jimmy stood, but nevertheless feeling elated and bubbly and with no regrets about the time they had just spent together – both had needed that release – Morgan made her way into the city early in the morning after only an hour or so sleep, rising, as she knew she would, from an empty bed. She had not expected to find Jimmy still there, but it didn't bother her. He would be back and they would talk.

Morgan had worked in a veterinary practice in east London for too many years but had always harboured dreams of possibly working in the financial sector. Her split from Jimmy had been the impetus for her to make the decision and now, two days a week, she worked from ten until three in a multinational insurance company in the square mile – basically as an office gofer. At the same time she was studying for her insurance examinations with a view, eventually, to becoming an insurance broker.

Her routine for those two precious days (the other five, she worked for the vet's) was to get into the city early and grab a coffee and an hour's study in a coffee house where she had become a regular face.

At eight that morning, she travelled in by bus – because she liked to see the city waking up, especially on a pre-winter's day like today. It was one of those special days when the sun rose languidly with a deceptively warm orange glow, silhouetting the buildings which pumped out smoke plumes from rooftop air ducts, pushing them high and wraithlike high into the sky.

She entered her usual café and was greeted by the waitress, Kerry, whom Morgan had got to know well over the past few months – someone else with a dream, but hers was to do with theatre, not finance.

'Hey Morgan – cappuccino?'

'Thanks. You know me so well.'

Morgan slid behind an empty table and pulled a file from her bag, placing the thick ring binder with her course notes in front of her.

The 40" flat screen TV on the wall, although turned on and tuned into a 24 hour news channel, wasn't really penetrating her thoughts as she opened the file. She was trying not to think how tired she was, just concentrated on the complex stuff she needed to learn.

Kerry arrived with the coffee, sliding the frothy brew onto the table.

Morgan smiled a thanks and Kerry said, gesturing to the TV, 'You heard about this? They've been on about it all morning, since I came on at six.' Morgan, feigning interest for the sake of politeness, raised her head and looked at the TV.

On screen, a reporter was enthusiastically gushing the news of an incident on some spare land in the docks. A large white crime scene marquee could be seen dramatically in the background, clearly covering something dreadful, while uniformed police and white suited CSIs and forensic evidence gatherers went about their allotted tasks. The reporter was standing on the public side of the stretched out crime scene tape.

'Well nobody really knows what Warren Evans was doing out here in the car on his own and we are yet to determine if he was actually alone,' the reporter said to camera. 'All we know is that there was a 999 call after a boat on the Thames saw the fire blazing…'

Kerry cut in then, voicing one of her many opinions. 'Who the hell cares, is what I say. Just some dealer who's pissed off one too many punters.'

'We do know that this particular area, just off the Colmore Road,' the reporter continued, 'is quite popular with teenagers and drug dealers and has been troublesome for some time…'

***

Another person listening to the words of the reporter, but standing in a group of about a dozen onlookers who were gawking at the scene, was Rob. He listened to her delivering her report to camera, then peeled away from the crowd and went to stand by the police cordon tape, looking at the tent and getting an occasional glimpse of the charred remains of

Warren's car as officers entered and left the tent, having to lift a flap as they did.

Rob took out his phone as he walked away from the scene.

***

Twenty minutes later, he had teamed up with Leon. They were threading their way through a maze of concrete stairs and walkways … their jungle.

Rob was slightly ahead, Leon having to speed up to keep with him.

Rob was a young man walking with a purpose: someone who had seen the evidence laid out before him, mulled it over, tried to make sense of it … and reached the only logical conclusion.

Leon, however, wasn't completely convinced. 'Yo, man, how can you be sure it was Caleb, man?'

Rob stopped abruptly. Leon almost collided with him.

'Who else it gonna be? You know them two spend most of their days arguing over percentages. Warren was only talking about offin' Caleb last week, man. You was there. You heard him.'

'Yuh,' Leon agreed. 'They argued like fuck, didn't they? It was gonna end bad, you could tell.'

'And that's why I know Caleb took Warren out … and Warren's ours, man, yeah?'

They turned into a stairwell and started making their way up the concrete steps.

'And now it's gonna end bad for Caleb.'

***

They reached the door of Caleb's flat unseen, unheard. Rob passed a pair of bolt cutters to Leon as they stood at the door, then Rob knocked.

'What?' Caleb asked from inside, his voice muffled.

'It's Rob, mate.' He was on the balls of his feet, trying to keep calm.

There was a pause, then the door opened to the length of the thick security chain, just enough of a gap for Caleb to squeeze his face into. 'What?' the big man demanded, his eyes distrustful.

'Let us in, fella. Wanna talk some business.' Rob's eyes, in their turn, could not look at Caleb's.

'Fuck off.'

Caleb did not do business with the likes of foot soldiers such as Rob or Leon. They were the ones who carried out the business as directed by him and people like Warren.

Caleb's face drew back from the gap. He made to shut the door, but Rob moved quickly, jamming his whole weight against the door to prevent it closing, snapping the chain rigid and surprising Caleb.

Leon brought up the bolt cutters, snipped the chain easily with the huge pincers and both lads forced the door, sending Caleb staggering backwards down the hall.

Rob screamed to Leon, 'Get his legs, pin the fucker down.' Rob knew that they would only get one chance at this – and it had to be done quick and hard. Leon fell over Caleb's thickly muscled legs and Rob dropped heavily across him, straddling his wide chest. His left hand went for the tattooed throat and his right hand shoved his pistol into Caleb's cheekbone, screwing it into the skin, and the line of tattooed teardrops cascading from Caleb's eye.

Although caught by surprise, Caleb remained icy cool. 'You better know what you're doing, mate,' he said through his distorted face, 'because when I get up, you two pricks are merked.'

'Tell me you didn't do it. TELL ME!' Rob screamed and slavered spittle into Caleb's face.

'What the fuck you bin takin', man? What you on about?'

'You fuckin' know – Warren.'

'Rob, you're trippin' out, Bruv. I ain't got a fuckin' clue what you're on about. Now,' – Caleb's voice dropped low, became ultra-dangerous – 'you got one chance to put that gun down and step off me and I'll let you both walk out of here alive. 'Cos whatever's happened to Waz, I ain't involved, blud.'

Caleb actually smiled through his twisted face, looking just beyond Rob's shoulder.

And Rob suddenly froze as he felt the unmistakeable muzzle of a shotgun press gently, but firmly against the back of his head.

He knew, without looking, who was holding it there.

If he had been able to look, he would have been treated to the vision that was Kadie, Caleb's girlfriend – an almost exact replica of him but scaled down and with huge tits and shaved pubes – standing there just in her bra, no panties, legs apart like a micro-colossus with a shaved head – looking down the barrel of a sawn-off, pump action shotgun as though she knew exactly what she was doing.

Actually, she did.

Rob said, 'Ain't even loaded.'

Kadie racked the weapon – click/clack, a sound that was terrifying – and fired a round just past Rob's head into the wall. She pumped the weapon again and pushed it back into his skull. 'You think?' she asked. 'Now get up, both of ya.'

She stepped back, covering the scene with a steady arc of the shotgun, but holding it mainly on Rob as he withdrew from his position across Caleb and clambered to his feet. He ensured he made no silly moves with his gun, anything that could have been misinterpreted. He knew Kadie would have no second thoughts in blasting a hole right through his chest.

Leon let go of the feet and stood up.

Caleb, rolled up, too.

Rob and Leon stood side by side at the door. 'Someone burnt out Warren's car,' Rob said defensively.

'With him in it,' Leon finished for him.

'What?' Caleb spat with disgust. 'And you thought that was me?' His voice turned to incredulity now. 'Why would I take the time to do something like that? I wanna off some prick, I put a bullet in him.' To emphasise this, Caleb made the shape of a gun with his right hand and pulled back his thumb as though cocking a hammer. He pointed at Rob.

They stared each other down, hard, ruthless individuals, caught in an inescapable circle of violence and retribution. Rob placed his forearm across Leon's chest and the two of them edged backwards a step, afraid to look away even for a moment.

But Rob still had the bottle to warn Caleb. 'We find out it's you, man...'

'Yeah, what?' the big man shouted. 'You ain't gonna do fuck all. Now fuck off and don't let me see either of you fuckin' clowns up on my block again.'

Leon backed out, followed by Rob.

***

Jimmy watched the screen of his laptop. Images taken from a CCTV camera.

At first he watched the events unfold and took pride in the stand that his father had taken against the robbery crew, defending rightfully what was his to defend. Then the swinging blow to the head of the young lad, Josh, who fell like a sack of shit. Clearly justified, just unfortunate that the lad died.

But, Jimmy thought, when you open a door and rob a shop, armed to the back teeth, you have to accept what comes back at you then, or later. The gang were the ones who set the agenda, not his dad, not Jimmy Vickers.

The CCTV footage was silent.

But Jimmy could imagine his dad's words.

After this, he watched it objectively, replaying, pausing – particularly the point at which the masked youth who looked as though he had been fleeing the shop had returned and faced his father, pointing at him with a knife. An unambiguous gesture. 'I will return. This business is not over.'

'Sure as hell ain't,' Jimmy muttered.

He replayed it all again, then froze the screen on the lad. He needed to absorb this, memorise it, get to know how this male walked, swaggered, every move, his clothes, absolutely everything.

In the end, Jimmy didn't need to see the face behind the mask.

***

The short day was coming to an end. The sun had tried, but its warmth had failed to penetrate London and there was now a real chill in the air.

Jimmy Vickers hunched down into his leather jacket.

He was in Greenwich Park, and behind him stood the magnificent statue of General James Wolfe, regally holding his telescope diagonally across his chest. He was one of Jimmy's heroes and the irony was not lost on him that Wolfe was both the victor and victim of the battle of Quebec in 1759, leading his men into a battle – the brilliant tactics for which he rightly took full credit – against the French. It was a bold plan, needing a lot of luck, but it worked. Unfortunately Wolfe was fatally wounded early in the battle, though he lived long enough to hear of his victory.

In the background, across the Thames, was the Isle of Dogs and City of London, now lit up as dusk came quickly.

Griff came up behind Jimmy, then stood alongside him.

Without acknowledgement, Jimmy pulled out a list of names that Warren had written for him. He handed it to his friend.

'I need addresses.'

Griff read the list, then – absently, but genuinely curious – he asked, 'Did it feel good?'

Jimmy looked at him for the first time. His expression did not actually change, but Griff saw the answer in his eyes: positive acknowledgement. It had felt good to kill Warren Evans. Then Jimmy looked away and said, 'There's four left.'

'Jimmy, you've got to let go, mate,' Griff appealed.

Jimmy smirked. 'What, and let you lot sort it? I got four names, what have you got?'

Griff's face tightened with his acknowledgement of the facts. The cops had nothing.

Without a word, Jimmy turned and walked away.

Griff stood there, not turning to speak to Jimmy's back, but saying, 'So this is it? Is this how it's gonna be? I stand back while you go on some urban killing safari across London?'

Jimmy stopped, turned, came back close to Griff. His voice was icy as cold steel in its resolve and certainty.

'You know as well as I do that this is the only way this is going to get done.' His nostrils dilated and he clenched his teeth for a second, grinding them, then speaking through them. He had worked it all out now, the rights, the wrongs, the consequences. 'And what happens if you do get one of them? Take a statement?' he mocked. 'Process them into the fuckin' criminal justice system, while they laugh at you, spit at you and then they get stuffed into a cosy prison cell where they can sit on their arse and play video games all fuckin' day? Them riots a few years back? That was a taster of what's to come. The country's changed, Griff.' Jimmy's voice took on an even darker tone. 'There was a time when I would bleed on the Union Jack to keep red in it. Them days are gone. We got a generation of offenders we don't know how to deal with, Griff.'

Griff had listened, his head tilted towards the sky, feeling more and more jittery as the truth of Jimmy's words gripped him. He turned and the two friends looked at each other. 'Then you know as well as I do, there's nothing to stop them from doing it again.'

Jimmy took a step forward. 'There's me.'

Griff's jaw rotated, fighting this. 'Revenge will never give you closure.'

'Revenge?' Jimmy sneered. 'This isn't revenge … not now … this is necessity.'

They stood eye to eye until Jimmy said, 'Get me an address,' and disappeared into the darkening gloom of the park, passing the statue of Wolfe, not even glancing up at it.

++++

Jimmy (Danny Dyer) leaves Warren trapped in a burning car

Rob (Josef Altin) prepares to confront Caleb over Warren's murder

NINE

Ronnie Holtz refilled the crystal glass from the very expensive bottle of red wine.

'That's enough for me.'

Holtz smiled. 'Not driving are you?'

'No, but I'm a lousy drunk.'

He placed the bottle back down and took a small sip of wine from his own glass, while eyeing the woman sitting opposite him. In a few words, she was tall, blonde and delicious. Holtz knew she had been a model for a while and made a lot of money at it. She was exquisite, elegant and the perfect accompaniment to the surroundings, one of London's top West End restaurants.

Holtz, too, looked as though he fitted in. His grey, thousand pound Italian cut suit that somehow never seemed to crease and always looked ultra-cool, was just right and covered Holtz like the best camouflage should, because in reality he was a cold-blooded predator and his prey that evening was the woman at this table – and the money behind her. He intended to fuck one and help himself to the other.

He sliced a chunk off his blood-oozing, perfectly cooked sirloin steak and almost groaned with pleasure as it disintegrated in his mouth. Then he sat back and surveyed this woman.

'Are you? Define lousy.'

'Well, put it this way,' she smiled, 'last time I got drunk I entered a wet T-shirt competition on holiday.'

Holtz grinned, felt his groin react at the thought of this woman's gorgeous breasts, visualising them in his hands, her nipples between his teeth. 'Is that right?'

'I won, of course,' she said, sat upright and slyly adjusted her position to gently push her breasts forward so they strained against her silk dress. Holtz felt himself move even more when he saw her nipples had hardened and grown, clearly visible against the material.

He swallowed. 'Obviously.'

She let her posture drop slightly and took a forkful of her vegetarian risotto.

Holtz topped up her glass again. She didn't raise her eyes but saw what he'd done and grinned naughtily to herself before looking up and asking him, 'What type of drunk are you?'

'I can be quite incorrigible.'

'Yeah,' she said, having her own thoughts, 'I imagine that mouth of yours get you into all sorts of trouble.'

'You make it sound like a bad thing. Unlike most people, I embrace the effects of alcohol. I certainly don't beat myself up about having a good time.'

'And this is your assessment of my character?'

'Not necessarily. But I can tell you're cautious, timid, sheepish, almost, in the face of a lovely glass of wine because you're terrified of that sexy little dress of yours ending up on my bedroom floor, your panties in my collection and my tongue licking your clit.'

'I'm not wearing panties,' she retorted, blushing coyly. Holtz knew he had hit the mark.

Their eyes levelled at each other and she reached for the very full glass of wine and swigged its entire contents in one. Holtz watched and raised his eyebrows.

She replaced the glass on the table, about to say something inappropriate, but stopped herself just in time as her husband, Alex, returned to the table, picked up his knife and fork, completely oblivious to the sexual interaction that had just taken place. He did, however, notice that his wife's wine glass was empty. He refilled it.

'Thirsty, Sophia dear?'

She glanced at Holtz.

Alex said, 'Sorry about that,' Referring to his absence from the table. 'Now, where were we?'

Holtz shifted uncomfortably and readjusted to being a businessman. This man – Alex – was the money behind Sophia and he was rich beyond Holtz's wildest dreams. And Holtz was interested in separating him from some of that fortune, more interested in that than screwing his wife, although that would be a nice bonus.

'I think we were about to come to thirty per cent, Alex, we were gonna shake on it and then move onto dessert. That's what your lovely wife was saying.'

'Ahh, was she now?' He raised his chin, pretending to be suspicious, but still having no clue about the sexual banter. He looked at Sophia admiringly. 'Well that's why I like to bring her along, Ronnie. Such a good judge of character, aren't you my darling?'

She smiled enigmatically.

Alex held her look, frowning, trying to read her, but nothing was forthcoming, so he made the decision and, turning to Holtz, he said, 'You got yourself a deal.'

The two men shook warmly and as they did, Holtz spotted a familiar figure perched on a barstool, clearly having observed the whole of the interplay. It was Jimmy Vickers, dressed appropriately for the surroundings in a black cashmere three-quarter-length coat, Chinos and brogues.

Holtz wiped his mouth with his napkin.

'If you guys will excuse me for a second.' As he stood, his napkin fell to the floor by Sophia's feet. Holtz stooped to pick it up and slipped his business card into Sophia's purse that hung on a gold chain down the side of her chair. It was a swift, almost unnoticeable move, but she saw it with a glance and a smile. Then Holtz moved away to the bar alongside Jimmy.

He snorted derisively. 'You know, it doesn't matter what you wear, Vickers, you still don't look right without an MP5 in your hands and an ammo rig across your chest like a fuckin' Mexican bandit.'

'I'll take that as a compliment.'

They smiled at each other, former comrades in arms, familiar but not friends and not close enough to shake hands on meeting. They kept a certain psychological distance between themselves, all the better to stay protected.

'She's something else,' Jimmy commented about Sophia.

Holtz flagged the barman, relieved it was no longer necessary for him to hide behind the smooth guy image, which he did so well. Jimmy knew a very different person behind the façade.

'So is her fella's wallet, mate. Get you a drink?'

Jimmy downed his Coke, implying another one would be good. When it arrived, Jimmy's tone became professional. 'I need to get my hands on some bits – if you're still in the business?' He pulled a folded piece of paper from his pocket and slid it along the bar. A shopping list.

Holtz read it, a serious expression on his face, his air of smoothness now having completely evaporated.

***

It was instantly cold as Jimmy, led by Holtz, stepped into the enormous walk-in refrigerator, in which hung rows and rows of huge, trimmed and gutted animal carcasses. Hundreds of cows, sheep and pigs, hanging silently and unmoving in frosted air rising from the chiller units. Holtz threaded through this slaughterhouse maze, Jimmy keeping with him, until they came to a huge metal desk in the far corner where a sleeping man sat with his feet up on the desk top, his ankles crossed, tilting back in a wide, comfortable office chair. The man was dressed in a huge duffel coat, probably with many layers underneath, a Ushanka hat on his head with the woollen flaps covering his ears and thick mittens on his hands.

His breath steamed out of his nostrils as he exhaled.

Holtz and Jimmy watched him for a few moments, the man Holtz knew as Trojan. He glanced at Jimmy, then nudged the man's chair.

Trojan's eyes shot open wide as he woke, startled and relieved to see it was Holtz waking him up.

'Ronnie.'

'Alright, Trojan?'

The man wiped his eyes with the back of his gloves. Despite the duffel coat and the under-layers bulking him out, Jimmy could see that Trojan was actually just a skinny streak of piss, looked like a good meal wouldn't go amiss and though he came across as edgy, there was a glint in his eyes that made Jimmy think he had a good heart.

***

Trojan led them further into the warehouse, from one refrigerated unit to another, until they finally reached their destination, a cold room about as far away from the main entrance as possible. Trojan opened a huge chest freezer and took out two stacking trays filled with meat cuts.

Jimmy and Holtz looked in at the selection of items laid out underneath where the meat had sat. An array of knives, all sizes, all uses.

Holtz reached in and picked out a Rambo-style knife with a ten inch blade. He held it up admiringly, then offered it to Jimmy.

'You're fuckin' jokin' ain't ya? Looks like Excalibur. I ain't walking round with that.'

'Just in,' Trojan said proudly. 'Titanium. That'll go through a car door.'

'Fuck do I want to stab a car for?'

Jimmy leaned into the freezer and selected a lock knife, smaller, more subtle, but equally deadly.

'That'll work too,' Trojan admitted.

Jimmy looked at Holtz, who was still admiring the Rambo knife, making slashing and stabbing motions like a kid. 'Put that away, will ya, before you have an eye out.'

'You wanna try that out?' Trojan asked Jimmy, nodding at the lock knife.

Jimmy screwed up his face, not understanding, and Trojan gestured to the hanging meat.

But Jimmy hesitated.

'Ever stabbed someone before?' Trojan asked but didn't wait for Jimmy to reply after getting a sidelong glance from him that told him he didn't want to hear the answer to that. Trojan set off to the nearest carcass and slapped it.

Jimmy and Holtz were behind him. Holtz nodded, 'This is the streets now, Jimmy. Different battlefield. Time for you to adjust.'

Jimmy assessed the meat.

Then a veil came down over his eyes and Jimmy Vickers stepped into the zone.

Holtz had witnessed this before. He stepped back cautiously, pulling a slightly mollified Trojan with him who opened his mouth to say something. Holtz silenced him with a glare.

Jimmy stepped up to the meat.

Images swept across his imagination. The indistinguishable faces of his parents' killers.

Then – snick, snick, snick – the knife slashed the meat with three well executed knife attacks.

'Again,' Holtz encouraged him.

This time Jimmy saw one face he did know: Warren's. It did not matter that he was already dead, because it gave Jimmy the focus he needed.

He rammed the knife into the meat again, seeing the terror on Warren's face, driven by it.

There then followed a series of slashes and blows as Jimmy's face became that of a demon again and he moved in a coordinated, supremely well-trained way with the grace and precision of a highly tuned athlete. He stabbed again and again and again, driving the final thrust up to the hilt and then stopped, his eyes ablaze.

Trojan gave Holtz a terrified look.

Jimmy stepped back and when Holtz saw his shoulders lose their tension he knew it was safe to speak.

'Not bad. Bit rusty.'

Jimmy turned, giving him a sardonic look while playing with the knife, locking it, unlocking it, whizzing it around and catching it by the handle like a cowboy twirling a six-shooter.

'Quite finished?' Trojan dared to ask. He led them into another cold room and opened a drawer in an old filing cabinet by the wall.

Inside hung a rack of handguns, a long row of them: Glock 17's, Glock 19's, HKP3000 and a Sig Sauer P226.

Jimmy reached in for the Sig.

Trojan said patronisingly, 'Now that's a Sig Sauer P226...'

Jimmy cut in mechanically. 'Takes fifteen 9mm calibre rounds in the clip, effective up to fifty metres ... in the right hands...'

Trojan nodded appreciatively. 'Man knows his toys.'

'Classic two-tone,' Jimmy went on. 'Stainless steel slide, polymer grips ... used by numerous law enforcement and military organisations worldwide, including US Navy Seals, the British Army ... the SAS. Takes fifteen 9mm rounds or twelve .357, weighs thirty-four ounces with the full magazine.' Jimmy weighed it up, a weapon very familiar in his hands. He had used one on many occasions, though the model and colour varied slightly.

Trojan handed him a loaded magazine.

Jimmy slotted it into the grip and cocked the slide, keeping the muzzle pointed to the floor.

Then he swivelled on the spot where he stood, adopted the classic combat stance, feet shoulder-width apart, knees slightly bent and brought the gun up in his right hand, cupping it with his left, making the weapon the acute angle of an isosceles triangle, elbows locked.

He had already chosen his target: a slab of meat about fifteen metres away from them.

Holtz instinctively covered his ears, knowing what was coming.

Trojan looked on, mesmerised.

The finger tip of Jimmy's right forefinger rested on the DA/SA trigger.

Then he fired fifteen continuous rounds into the carcass. It wasn't fancy shooting. None of that holding the weapon sideways and parallel to the ground gangster crap. It was fast, efficient and effective, learned and drilled in and practised and then practised again in a multitude of conditions, until the practice became second nature and firing this type of weapon, and many other types, became an integral part of who Jimmy Vickers was and what he became.

Then, the shooting done, he lowered the weapon, the cordite rising and the sound reverberating around the room until the ringing died away and all that could be heard was the electric hum of the refrigerators.

Holtz slowly unpeeled his hands away from his ears. Trojan, temporarily deaf, looked on – still mesmerised.

Fifteen metres away, the carcass of a cow had been shredded.

Jimmy looked critically at his handiwork. He hadn't wanted to impress, had just needed the release and – yes, maybe – the confirmation that he still had it, even though he knew he had.

Holtz said, 'We'll take it.'

Trojan, whose hearing had returned, said, 'I'll get you a silencer for that.'

***

Holtz paid cash and Trojan gave them both a wave before returning to his reclining position at his desk.

At the warehouse exit, Holtz laid a hand on Jimmy's arm.

'You should know that's not me any more, Jimmy,' he said, wafting a hand at the warehouse. 'I'll dip my toe in now and again to help out a pal. That's all. My life has moved on.'

'Appreciate it.'

The two men hesitated. Jimmy made to go, but Holtz stopped him gently. Jimmy saw it coming: speech time. He hoped he wouldn't have to tell Holtz to fuck off. The last thing he needed was a lecture.

It wasn't.

'Listen Jimmy, we've been through the shit, the blood and the mud together. Bullets zingin' over our heads like they're going out of fuckin' fashion – but that look I saw in your eye, it ain't good, Jimmy mate.'

'I got it under control.'

Holtz's face softened – and Jimmy realised that he knew it all. 'I feel your pain, sunshine and I get all of that "the police ain't gonna do nothing so I gotta stand up and do it myself" business. I'd be doin' the same. But I meant what I said back there, man. This is a different battlefield,' he warned Jimmy – who was listening because he respected this man and owed his life to him on a couple of occasions, just as Holtz owed his life to Jimmy. 'You wanna take a stand out there, you got to be tall. Taller than you've ever been before. People wanna hide in their living rooms with their infomercials, eating sixty-seven flavours of crisps, wanting to see if anyone'll comment on their status update while the world fuckin' burns at their doorsteps. There's more crimes than coppers. These streets are lawless, man.' He paused and Jimmy sensed the guy's heightened emotions. 'The difference with fighting in the desert and here is that over there you're actually surrounded by people who have your back and give a shit. Here...'Holtz let the speech fade with a hopeless gesture. Jimmy took it in, then Holtz shrugged and said, 'You need anything else, you give me a shout ... come here.'

Holtz offered his hand and the two men shook, then hugged before Jimmy broke away, turned, left.

Holtz watched him go, wondering if he would ever see him again.

++++

Jimmy (Danny Dyer) thanks Ronnie (Nick Nevern) for supplying him with weapons for his crusade

Jimmy Vickers (Danny Dyer) uses Rob (Josef Altin) as a human shield in his raid on Caleb's den

TEN

Jimmy Vickers was immune to the frustrations of waiting. No one could teach anyone how to wait. It was one of those things that just had to be done and could only be self-taught. Some of the best soldiers that he knew could not stand waiting, hated it with a vengeance. Did their heads in – but it wasn't an option not to wait and they had to learn to deal with it in their own way.

For Jimmy, he simply went into himself. Withdrew into his mind and worked things out and through.

He had once spent four days solid in a fox hole in Helmand, a scraping no deeper than a man, laid out full length on his belly, covered in sand and grit as camouflage. Unable to move for fear of revealing his position. Hardly able to breathe, and having to piss down a catheter inserted into his penis. Having a shit was out of the question, so four days of Imodium meant his guts were as solid as a brick wall. All he had to survive on was tepid water and mushed up vitamin drinks, fed to him via a plastic straw from a container on his belt.

At the end of that stint, he'd had to move as quickly as though he'd warmed up for exercise and pretend that his limbs and muscles were ready for action. There was no chance of pleading with the enemy to 'hold on a mo' while I just stretch off first'.

But the wait and the discomfort had been ultimately worth it, when the Intel that Jimmy had gathered proved correct. A small, very mobile, much feared Taliban unit appeared and set up camp – only to suddenly find themselves surrounded by eight dusty SAS soldiers who rose from their holes like zombies rising alive from the grave, and attacked them.

It was over in seconds.

Four days funnelled into a thirty-second fire fight.

Twelve dead Taliban and no injury on the SAS side.

The first thing Jimmy had then done was to have that excruciating shit of relief, much to the mocking of his fellow officers – who all then followed suit.

So tonight, under the shadow of a council tower block, a four hour wait for his prey to emerge, while sitting in a heated car, scoffing shop-bought sandwiches and coffee from a flask, was nothing.

The equivalent of staying in a five star hotel.

His prey was just as dangerous, though maybe less cunning than a Taliban warrior. As shown when Danny Cross came out of the ground floor foyer of the block and jogged openly, as though he didn't have a care in the world, to a car parked across the road.

Jimmy watched him, comparing him to the photograph he had obtained. A match.

Danny pulled away in the car, Jimmy followed in the 4x4.

***

Three shot glasses were lined up on the bar top. Terry filled them with vodka, keeping a cautious eye on the three young men in front of him. A wary eye – and a frightened one.

Danny took his glass and held it up, as did the other two, Rob and Leon.

'For Waz,' Danny toasted sincerely.

The others saluted with their glasses and all three downed their shots simultaneously. Danny grimaced as the foul taste of the cheap, potent liquor hit the spot.

'Get some more in, boys – I need a piss.'

Rob slid a tiny bag of white powder surreptitiously to Danny. ''Ere, get a grab on this.' Danny palmed the drugs and glanced at Terry behind the bar, who had seen the move. Danny shot him a challenging look. Terry looked away spinelessly. Danny smirked cockily, then headed for the toilets.

Leon ordered fresh shots with just a movement of his eyes, leaned on the bar and asked Rob, 'Thought who it could have been yet?'

'Nah, man. You?'

The drink had already entered Rob's system and he was well on the way to being smashed. He leaned into Leon, grabbed him around the back of the neck and pulled him close so their foreheads touched.

'Fuck knows who it was, Bruv. But we'll find 'em, and when we fuckin' do, me, you and that scrawny little shit in there will fuckin' ruin 'em, Yeah?'

Terry had refilled the shots.

***

Danny stepped out of the toilet cubicle, wiping his nose with his thumb and forefinger, sniffing, having just nostril-hoovered up the contents of the plastic bag from the shiny surface of the toilet cistern. He crossed to the row of sinks and ran a tap, not having seen the figure by the door.

The man was dressed completely in black, with a three-holed balaclava pulled over his head. Strips of pre-cut grey duct tape had been stuck across his jacket.

Danny still hadn't seen him as he swilled his hands and turned to the roller-towel on the wall to his left, tugging down a length.

Then his sixth sense kicked in and he became aware of the menacing figure. He frowned, turned sharply.

The man did not move, simply stared through the eye holes at Danny.

'Got a fuckin' problem, mate?'

No response from the black-clad figure, who remained still, unmoving.

Danny was uncertain – and not a little scared by the presence, because a balaclava still remained one of the most terrifying psychologically superior moves that a criminal could make. From the Black Panther to the common armed robber, the sight of a balaclava on a villain's head successfully struck real fear into victims and witnesses. And even other crims. Danny responded in the only way he knew – by going aggressive.

'I said, you got a problem?' he snarled.

The masked man advanced. Fast.

Danny panicked, trying to hide his fear, and cajoled, 'Come on, then,' and once the figure was in range he swung a punch. But not a good one. It was wet, weak and telegraphed. The masked man simply ducked and sidestepped to avoid it and unleashed his own massive, leather fisted punch into Danny's face, and moved in. Danny grabbed him and fought desperately, but the man was relentless, clinical and overpowering. At one point he crashed an elbow into Danny's face, sending him spiralling backwards against the wall, cracking his head on the corner of the towel dispenser.

Gamely, Danny came back at him, but his legs had gone and the masked man easily turned him and ran his face against the towel dispenser again, catching Danny's right nostril on the sharp bottom corner of it and ripping it away from his face.

Danny screamed, lost all his fight and slithered half-conscious down the wall, leaving a smear of blood.

The masked man moved in quickly, ripping a strip of duct tape from his jacket, covering Danny's mouth with it. Then a second strip was wrapped tight around his wrists, a third around his ankles. He was trussed up in seconds.

***

The night was bright and cold. A full moon helped to illuminate an otherwise dimly lit section of a derelict warehouse through broken skylights.

Danny sat in the centre of the concrete floor, tied to an old, metal framed chair. His legs were taped to the chair legs, his arms pulled tight behind his back, bound at the wrists.

Tape had also been wound around his forehead and was now holding Danny's head back, angled towards the warehouse roof. He could not see anything, because a length of tape covered his eyes.

He tried to gasp and swallow, but he could not close his mouth. It was being held open by a dental mouth clamp that had been screwed open to its limit so Danny's mouth was as wide open as it possibly could be – and because of the angle at which his head had been pinned back, it was a perpendicular, unobstructed journey from his mouth, down his throat, through his chest and into his guts.

Jimmy ripped the tape off Danny's eyes, tearing out his eyebrows and eyelashes, making Danny moan – in a gargling sort of way. The noise was more a whimper of terror and he tried to look around, but his view was restricted and he was totally unable to move, despite trying.

Jimmy came in close for Danny to see him.

His first message was a terrifying one.

'You're gonna die tonight, fella.'

Danny squirmed and tried to emit a 'Nooo' sound, which came out more like a sea lion calling for a fish.

'Yeah, yeah,' Danny said conversationally. 'Yeah you are, I'm afraid, mate.'

Jimmy moved out of Danny's area of vision. He continued to chat. 'Reason why it ain't happened yet is that your current unfortunate position leaves me severely spoilt for choice.'

He stepped back and loomed over Danny while easing on a pair of latex gloves, ensuring that Danny saw this.

'Because I could pretty much put anything in there.' He bent forwards and peered with one eye into the cavity that was Danny's mouth. Then he talked into the gaping hole.

'Hello?' he called. He paused, then faked an echo. 'Hello … hello … hello…' His voice became a whisper. He stood up. 'Sorry, bad joke.'

Danny started to cry with big, choking sobs. In his pocket his mobile phone vibrated, then started to ring. Danny reached in and pulled it out. The caller display simply read, 'Rob.'

Jimmy thumbed the answer call button. Said nothing, just listened.

He heard Rob's voice. 'Dan? Danny mate? Stop fuckin' us about. We're worried, fella.'

Rob was making the call from the front steps of The Wolf, standing alone, pacing back and forth.

'So you fuckin' should be.'

'Who the fuck is this? Where's Danny?'

Jimmy glanced at him. 'He can't talk just now.'

'Who are you, mate?' Rob demanded.

Jimmy didn't respond.

Then it became clear to Rob. 'You're the guy that did Warren! What's your fuckin' problem?'

Again Jimmy did not reply, purposely racking up the tension in Rob. Using silence, such an effective but little used tool.

'I said, what's your problem?' Rob demanded again, the inflection in his voice rising as he became more agitated.

'Deserved to burn, your mate,' Jimmy said at last. 'For what he did. What you all did to that couple.'

It was Rob's turn to stay silent as he digested the words. 'About that?' he asked incredulously. 'What the fuck's that gotta do with you?'

Jimmy said nothing.

Rob snarled, 'Think you're fuckin' scary, do ya? On the other end of a phone? Fuckin' scary man, aren't you? Well let's go face to face, see how scary you are then. Where are ya?'

Jimmy lowered the tone of his voice, composing himself as adrenaline surged through his body. His face became deadly blank as he said, 'We will go face to face, and when I see you, I am going to annihilate you...' Then he said it slowly, emphasising each word, each syllable, so that the meaning was clear. 'I … am … going … to … annihilate … you.'

He pressed the end call button, dismantled the phone, throwing it onto the floor, crushing it with his heel.

He inhaled a steadying breath.

Then he bent down next to a bucket and said to Danny, 'You're gonna love this, mate. A little lesson on cement.'

He glanced at his captive and saw the spreading puddle of piss forming underneath the chair and smelled the shit as Danny's bladder and bowels evacuated with fear.

The bucket did contain cement and Jimmy stirred it with a stick, continuing with his promised lesson. 'In the most general sense of the word, cement is a binder, a substance that sets and hardens independently and can bind other materials together. The word cement actually comes from the Romans who used the term 'opus caementicium' to describe masonry resembling modern concrete that was made from crushed rock with burnt lime as a binder.' Jimmy continued to stir, getting the consistency in the bucket just right. 'And there was an earlier version of cement used in Mesopotamia in the third millennium BC and later in Egypt. It has a fascinating history for such a common, everyday substance. One of those things nobody gives a shit about until it crumbles.'

The mixture was right for him now.

He asked Danny, 'Ever heard of Foie-gras?'

Danny, gagging, struggling to breath and swallow, made a horrible gurgling noise.

'Probably no, then, a fuckin' heathen like you. But let me tell you something about it – because it's just as relevant as cement to this process we're going to be going through.'

Jimmy crossed over to Danny and set the bucket of cement down by the side of the chair, lifting the stick out of it and watching it drip back.

'Bit of a culture lesson, eh? Before you die.' He continued stirring. 'Foie-gras, in case you didn't know, is French for fat liver, a product made from the liver of a goose or duck that has been specially fattened. And d'you know how they do it? They force feed the animal with corn, using what they call a gavage, and basically what they do is put a funnel into the goose's mouth and then tip food into it and squeeze it all the way down its neck. Particularly fuckin' cruel if you ask me but very apt today, especially where you're concerned. I say cruel because a goose doesn't have a choice in the matter, but, mate, you did have a choice. And you chose very badly.'

Jimmy stood in front of Danny.

'Now as it happens, I don't have a gavage, but I do have a piping bag, which'll just have to do instead.'

Jimmy held up a large nylon piping bag, the type used by chefs to decorate cakes with icing. 'It's a sturdy one and should be okay.'

He began to spoon the sloppy cement into the bag until it was full, then he tied the top and took the metal cover off the opening and placed it into Danny's mouth – and started to squeeze the cement out.

Panicking desperately, Danny tried to spit it out and wriggle free, using all his strength, but Jimmy was relentless, forcing it down his throat.

'I'm fucking good at decorating cakes, too,' he said grimly.

++++

ELEVEN

'Wow!'

DCI Spencer Holland tapped his knuckles on the levelled off, hardened cement in Danny Cross's mouth. His own face screwed up distastefully.

A crime scene photographer's camera flashed.

'Wow,' Holland said again and tapped once more. 'Rock solid.' He glanced around at the police activity in the derelict warehouse. The forensic suited staff at work, the uniformed officers on the other side of the tape that had been strung up to preserve the scene. A lighting rig powered by a portable generator had been erected and switched on, because even though it was daylight now, very little natural light filtered through the skylights and there was no electricity connected to the place.

Holland, being his usual arrogant self, had bowled in and refused to kit up, wanting to get to the vortex of the action immediately.

He stood away from Danny's body, having at least the sense to avoid stepping into the two words scraped into the concrete floor at Danny's feet: 'THREE LEFT.' Holland considered the words while looking thoughtfully through slitted eyes at PC Jenny Clarke as she approached him. Unlike Holland, she was in a disposable forensic suit.

'Group of kids found him,' she explained.

Holland shook his head, nonplussed. 'Where the bloody hell do you start with something like this?' he muttered to himself as though he hadn't heard Clarke's piece of information.

There was a metallic object on the floor nearby that had been tagged and numbered and by which one of the CSI team had laid a twelve inch ruler so that when the photographs were printed and processed, the size of the object could be understood. Holland grimaced, 'What is that?'

'A mouth clamp. Dentist's use 'em, so do throat surgeons.'

'Looks like some sort of sex toy,' he said quietly and turned to Clarke with a dirty grin, expecting her to reciprocate. Her face remained deadpan – because she detested the man. He left her feeling cold and queasy.

The DCI then ran his open hands up and down Danny's chest and stomach. He pressed.

'Fuckin' solid.'

'One of the forensic guys says he might have swallowed up to two litres before he eventually suffocated. The cement has bound all his internal organs together,' Clarke said. 'If you whacked him with a sledgehammer now, he'd probably break like a statue. The post mortem's gonna be fun.'

'Fuck me.'

'Serious Crimes are on their way, incidentally, sir,' Clarke informed Holland.

'Fuck that – I'm all over this. I've been dying for something a bit unusual to fall into my lap since I got promoted, love. I'm not handing this over to anyone.'

Holland tore off his jacket, tossed it to Clarke to catch, rolled up his shirt sleeves and snapped a pair of latex gloves on, his eyes fired up with over-enthusiasm, staring at Danny's rigid body. He spoke to Clarke without looking in her direction. 'You get the statements from the kids and rustle us up some coffee, love. Gonna be a long day.'

She looked at him with the word 'twat' on her lips – thought but unsaid – and headed off, bearing his jacket.

In his trouser pocket, Holland's phone rang.

***

Holland stepped into the main bar of The Wolf. He surveyed the premises with an air of distaste. Definitely not his sort of place. Low class and shitty. Wouldn't be seen dead in it, not unless he was here to solve a murder.

He hunched his shoulders and went to the bar, flashing his ID to Debbie, the barmaid.

'DCI Holland,' he announced smoothly. 'A colleague of mine informs me you have something on your CCTV I need to look at.'

The vibes from this woman – this old tart, Holland thought – were not good. She regarded him with a curl on her pouting lips. 'Not me, love.'

'Well somebody from this pub rang the police and here I am, as if by magic,' he said facetiously.

Terry stepped out from the back room.

'Was me … I rang ya.'

Debbie looked at Terry with much more than annoyance on her face.

***

There was a small office at the back of the main bar and on a shelf, side by side, were three small TVs, all with blank screens.

Terry rewound a tape on an old VHS VCR and cued it up. As the tape ran, the three TV screens came to life, showing a view from three cameras set up discreetly to cover the rear of the pub, stacked beer barrels, crates and other debris associated with the backs of pubs all over the country. The pictures themselves, though, were quite fuzzy and in black and white. Clearly this surveillance set-up had been done on the cheap.

'Had these installed last year,' Terry explained to Holland, who stood just behind him, impatience oozing from every pore. Debbie hovered at his shoulder.

She put in, pointedly, sarcastically, 'Mainly because after the last set of break-ins we had, you lot said you couldn't really do anything.'

Holland scowled and suppressed the urge to say, 'Whatever.' Instead, he just said 'Right, okay,' and looked like he was stifling a yawn. He was 'up to here' with hearing this particular whinge against the police. They couldn't be fucking everywhere, could they?

But Debbie was on one. 'Too busy sitting in warm offices doing paperwork, I expect.' She folded her arms under her ample bosom and Holland thought, 'Please don't do a Les Dawson on me.' But she ploughed on, 'Processing criminals instead of giving the little fuckers what they really need – a good kicking.'

'Paperwork and procedure are the bane of the current police service, I assure you,' Holland threw her the party line. 'We are always looking at ways of reducing the burden, trying to keep the uniforms on the streets as much as possible…'

'And another thing…' she started.

'Debbie,' Terry said tetchily, glaring at her, raising his eyebrows. Her breasts pushed up against her blouse and she folded her arms more tightly.

But she snapped, 'Can I have a word, Terry?'

Terry glanced at Holland, who gave a sympathetic shrug, then eased past the detective into the bar behind Debbie.

'What?' he demanded, even though he knew.

'What exactly are you doing?' she asked hoarsely.

'Protecting my pub.'

'Your pub?' she said with disbelief. 'We both know exactly who you're protecting ... is this out of fear?'

Terry looked past her absently, like a chastened schoolboy, his mouth pouting like a cat's arse. His whole demeanour was sheepish and ashamed. He had been caught out.

'You know exactly who that car belongs to. You can't turn a blind eye?'

Terry's voice rasped. 'Those twats know everything, Debs. They get wind I let this slip and this place goes up in flames, us in it probably. You've seen what they can do. They're wild animals.'

Debbie looked deeply into his eyes, tried to keep her voice low. 'And I know what Jimmy Vickers can do ... he's gonna steamroller the lot of 'em. Just let him get on with it. Do not give him up to that shark in there.'

Terry hesitated.

Debbie went on remorselessly, 'Terry, I have never met a more cowardly man than you.'

He was about to respond and defend his position when Holland – now at the end of his patience tether – stuck his head around the door. 'You said you had something for me?'

It broke the moment and when Terry turned and went back in, Debbie shook her head in frustration and clenched her fists.

Terry eased himself past Holland, fiddled with the VCR controls and hit the play button.

The grainy images showed a black 4x4 reverse up to the back of the pub and stop. A figure climbed out and entered the pub via the back door.

'There,' Terry said.

'So what?' Holland shrugged. 'Bloke gets out of a car, goes into a pub. Sounds like the start of a shit joke.'

'This is no joke,' Terry assured him.

Debbie stepped up and looked at the screens between the shoulders of the two men. 'You can't see anything,' she said, hoping to head them off. 'That CCTV is as old as you are.'

Terry tutted and fast-forwarded the tape, saying, 'Twenty minutes later, this.'

A masked man appeared on screen, carrying a body over his shoulder like a rolled up carpet. The body was slung into the back of the 4x4. The man got into the car and drove off.

Holland watched, open-mouthed – seeing this all play out in front of him: one hell of a brilliant arrest. Then he said, 'But shit, the angle's too high to get the plates ... need to rewind...'

He lurched forward and pressed rewind, back to the point where the car originally reversed in. He froze the screen at the moment the man climbed out, then leaned more closely to peer at the dark figure.

Debbie closed her eyes as Holland uttered, 'Got you, you fucker.'

***

The particular 'fucker' Holland was referring to was, at that moment, running alone, leaning into a slight gradient. His route was not especially tortuous, nothing approaching a route march in the Brecon Beacons, but it was enough to put him through some pain and a bit of therapy, too.

And the second time around the perimeter of Hyde Park would test the endurance of anyone, no matter how fit.

His first circuit had been just over five miles and he was over halfway through the second, pushing hard, punishing himself, checking his wristwatch to see how long he was taking, upping the pace, pounding hard down Rotten Row, the 28lb rucksack on his back now starting to feel heavy, even though it was nowhere near as weighty as the equipment he'd often had to carry for many miles over treacherous terrain. What he was doing here was, almost literally, a walk in the park.

Or, actually, a run in the park.

A 10.24 mile run.

But it was enough.

He had needed it to help him deal with the emotional aftermath of a mortal contact. The blood pounding through his veins helped him to filter his system, come clean again.

He pushed himself harder now, approaching the end.

His powerful muscles, toned by a combination of exercise and hard daily routine, now started to scream as he upped the pace, merciless with himself for the last half mile as he reached Palace Gate and slowed, warming down, then stopped and spent fifteen minutes stretching, consuming over a litre of water and then returning to normal. And feeling physically great.

All the while, he watched for the watchers.

He was satisfied there were none. Not here, anyway, not unless they were very much better than he, though he wasn't foolish enough to believe that there weren't better people out there. There was always someone better. That's how it was.

He trotted over Kensington Road and into the streets of South Kensington where he had managed to find a parking space for the Hi-Lux. He had left his tracksuit in the car and he put it on while at the same time slyly checking the vehicle, its underside and wheel arches, for any signs of a tracker device. Or worse.

Nothing.

But he knew he didn't have long. Just for the moment, Jimmy Vickers was ahead of the pack, but soon they would be snapping at his heels. He slid into the car and started the engine. Now he needed to get back to his apartment and get a long, hot shower.

He drove east through the city, actually enjoying the slowness of the heavy traffic, giving him more time to think and keep track of any possible surveillance.

As the traffic thinned and he entered his home territory, passing The Wolf on his right, he spotted the first out of place car. An unremarkable Astra, parked down one of the side streets, two men on board. Just sitting there, parked up.

Out of place.

Jimmy's senses clicked up a few notches and an empty feeling came to his lower guts.

He drove on, not even glancing at the car, but keeping his eye on his door mirror to see if the car pulled out and started to follow him.

It didn't.

Jimmy reached under the driver's seat and found the handle of the Sig, then placed it between his thighs, but out of sight.

His eyes narrowed, trying to slot it all together.

Maybe it wasn't the cops. Maybe it wasn't anybody.

But Jimmy Vickers hadn't survived for so long in hostile environments by making assumptions about anything. If it had stripes and pointy teeth and claws and it roared and looked like a tiger, treat it like a tiger, was Jimmy's motto. Don't try and grab the fucker by the tail unless you had to, and only then if you had a blunderbuss in your hand.

He drove on.

And saw the next car. This time parked discreetly at the back of a piece of derelict land used as an unofficial car park.

Same model as the last one. Same dull colour, even. Two men on board.

'Shit,' he said, drove on, didn't stop.

It was a tiger.

***

Morgan opened the front door of her house to two uniformed cops. One was Jenny Clarke, the other a PC called John Taylor.

'Mrs Vickers?' Clarke asked.

Morgan nodded. 'Yes.' It was a statement and also a question. She could not help but look worried. At the best of times, two cops on the doorstep was not a good sign, and not very long ago Morgan had answered a similar knock and been informed of the horrific death of Jimmy's parents.

PC Taylor, younger even than Clarke, said, 'It's about your husband, Mrs Vickers. James Vickers.'

'Yes?' Morgan sounded mystified.

'Have you seen him in the last few days at all?'

'No, I haven't.'

Clarke leaned in and glanced over Morgan's shoulder. 'Not at all? Are you sure?'

'Look, what is this about?' Morgan asked crossly.

'We have reason to believe he has been involved in a number of serious crimes.'

'Like what?' Morgan asked. Suddenly her heart rammed and the pulses in the side of her head pounded, like her skull was going to explode.

Clarke said, 'I'm sorry, we can't say.'

'But if you see him, you need to give us a call as soon as possible.' Taylor handed Morgan a business card. 'This is the name and number of DCI Holland, the officer in charge of this investigation.'

Morgan took it.

'Call him, or treble-nine the police,' Clarke said. 'We need to find your husband urgently.'

Morgan nodded, closed the door and the pair turned to leave.

***

She slowly made her way back into the kitchen, dragging her feet which now felt like clay. The kitchen blinds were drawn and Jimmy Vickers sat at the table, still dressed in his tracksuit. She walked past him and stood by the sink, holding herself in check by looking away from him, but then she spun accusingly.

'Those murders … on the TV news … they're you, aren't they?'

Jimmy sat at the table, his fingers interlocked in front of him, his head bowed. He had no adequate reply for her.

Suddenly she flipped, and swept a mug and a glass flying off the sink drainer, sending them spinning through the air before crashing and smashing onto the tiled floor, glass and ceramic shards bursting everywhere.

She ground her teeth, 'Can't you just leave things alone?'

Jimmy had not moved, but now he turned his face slowly towards her and she became horrified by the killing expression on his face, a dark shadow having come to his eyes … evil, almost. Like nothing she had ever seen before.

'Morgan,' he said matter-of-factly, 'they executed my parents.'

'And you doing this? What's that, revenge? It sure isn't justice.'

'Them bastards don't deserve to live. Don't deserve justice. They need their hearts tearing out, all of them.'

Unable to take or listen to any more of this, or deal with it, Morgan clamped her fists to her head, drumming her temples as she stormed out of the room.

Jimmy bent down and began to collect the broken pottery and glass.

***

Jimmy stood at the window of Morgan's bedroom. Night had fallen and from this darkened room, he peered through a sliver of a gap at the edge of the drawn curtains, careful not to move them. He was focused on something in the street.

Morgan came in.

'They've been out there all day. Waiting for you to turn up, no doubt.' She sat on the edge of the wide, king size bed. Her voice had softened and she was much more laid back now. Jimmy stepped away from the window.

Morgan took her weight on her hands, leaning back, her head shaking slightly as she said, 'When they told me what had happened, I couldn't believe it. Who does that to an innocent couple? I just wanted to find you...'

Jimmy kept looking at her.

She said, 'What did you do, Jimmy?'

Jimmy realised the time had come for answers. He knew he had so much to thank her for, taking the burden of the deaths of his parents and arranging everything that followed that he should have been home to sort out, but wasn't. There had been no obligation for her to do this. Even though his mum and dad had treated and loved her as though she had been their own flesh and blood, she had no ties or responsibility to them now because she and Jimmy had split, were getting divorced.

She had done it simply for love. For them. For him.

And he didn't deserve it.

He now realised that she had spent too many years trying to figure out the mind of a husband she would never understand, who was always away fighting dirty wars in dirty places, dedicated to his country more than to his wife.

The test of time had put a burden on their relationship that eventually broke it.

And now, here in that bedroom, Jimmy realised he had thrown away the one constant in his life: Morgan. And she merited some answers for once. An insight into the mind of a man she loved but could never fully comprehend.

He moved to her side and sat next to her, his eyes and mind looking into the distance – or the past – trying to make sense of it himself.

'Afghan soldiers we were training turned on our guys,' he said quietly, recalling it all with pain. 'Five Taliban killed six

113

British soldiers. We needed to figure out if there were any more among us, so they put me to work.'

Morgan watched him talking, studied him, searching for that insight, but also realising that he had dropped his guard and was vulnerable now. His eyes were moist as he spoke, tears close.

'This one guy … I got him talking … he fuckin' would have done us all. He knew so much … I couldn't let him live, Morgan. I had to try and hold Mickey Burton's face together because of people like him. So I ended him. Went too far … and they locked me up.'

'And you escaped?'

Jimmy gave a snort and nodded. 'You could say that.'

Morgan took his left hand, feeling closer to him than she had ever done in their entire marriage. She took hold of the wedding ring he persisted in wearing and rolled it between her finger and thumb.

He glanced down. 'I do that a lot.'

'Was there ever anyone else?' she whispered fearfully.

He shook his head, looked down at his thighs, his thoughts and memories returning to a brutal, faraway place.

Morgan reached up to his face with the palm of her hand and gently turned him towards her as she slid up tight next to him. For a moment their faces were close, their eyes playing over each other, searching. Then she kissed him.

**

Daylight cut through the narrow gap in the curtains.

Morgan lay on her front under the white sheet, her head resting on the pillow, her bare back and shoulders lit by the pale shaft of sunlight. Her skin was fine, pale and flawless.

Jimmy perched on the corner of the bed, watching her sleeping, entranced by her beauty. She stirred, opened her eyes and smiled. In the very early days of her marriage, Jimmy had often watched her as she slept and she had found it lovely, reassuring, as though he were watching over her. She slid over to him, running her fingertips up his body, touching the knife wound she had sewn and was healing well already. She traced it with the tip of her forefinger and it made her think gloomy thoughts.

'This can only end badly,' she predicted.

'What's the alternative?'

'Get in a car and drive until you run out of fuel?' she grinned. 'You might have to, yet.'

'Would you come with me?' he asked hesitantly. Maybe he had misjudged her, but she nodded. He said, 'I have to finish this first.'

Now she knew that. Understood it. She nodded again and said, 'Yes.'

He rose slowly, walked into the en suite shower room, closed the door.

Morgan licked her lips, thinking. Then she rolled sideways and opened the top drawer of her bedside cabinet. She dipped her fingers in and took out her wedding ring.

She slid it onto her finger.

++++

Holland (Alistair Petrie) inspects Jimmy's gruesome execution of Danny (Sam Hudson)

Morgan Vickers (Roxanne McKee) shares a tender moment with her estranged husband Jimmy (Danny Dyer)

TWELVE

There is no doubt about it – there are still a lot of good cops out there. Cops who joined the job for the right reason and who take pride in developing and honing their skills; cops who are good thief takers and who don't want to climb an increasingly corporate ladder but want to spend their days unburdened by unnecessary paperwork and out on the streets, making the bricks theirs and catching crims.

Such a cop was PC John Taylor.

He was young – in years and service – but he had very early on decided that his future was catching villains and putting them away.

In his patch in east London he had already built a reputation as being fair and firm – he was no hothead – and as someone who would work hard for victims and witnesses, treating them with compassion and empathy and would always crack down and be on the lookout for criminals and wanted persons.

One of the things he prided himself on was his prodigious memory and ability to recognise faces – a skill vital to a good cop.

However, the only picture that he'd seen of the man the cops were hunting at that exact moment in time (a 'squaddie' he'd been derisively called by DCI Holland, the lead investigator, at that morning's briefing, 'some freakin' nut job allegedly suffering from post-traumatic stress syndrome, more like PMT if you ask me,') had been a grainy still downloaded from a poor CCTV snapshot.

It was a bad photo by any standards, a fuzzy three-quarter close–up of a man in the back yard of a pub.

Taylor had studied it closely.

Squinting at it, turning his head, trying to work out exactly what this man – the information about whom was sketchy to say the least – really looked like.

He did also wonder why the gen on this James Vickers guy was so sparse. The military authorities were usually quick and helpful in supplying information to the police about soldiers.

But for some reason, not James Vickers.

Which puzzled Taylor, but still did not put him off in having some part in bringing the guy in, although he did acknowledge it would be unlikely for him, a mere PC working on the periphery of an intense investigation, to have any chance at all at catching the fucker.

There was every chance, Taylor thought, that Vickers would end up with a laser sight hovering on his chest and then having his heart blasted out.

It had been a long morning for Taylor and his colleague for the day, PC Addison, an even younger cop. Their role was simply to sit in a car, keep obs, and hope. It was a vague strategy, to say the least, because Taylor thought it would have been much easier and straightforward to kick down Morgan Vickers's front door and raid her house.

In his short service, Taylor had learned how to spot liars, even good ones. He was certain that Morgan Vickers was a liar – and a bad one at that – and when he'd spoken to her briefly the previous day, he was unimpressed by her shifty eyes and guilty body language.

She'd said she hadn't seen Jimmy.

Instantly, Taylor had tagged that as a lie. He thought the cops should have returned en masse and searched her house, but his voice went unheeded by DCI Holland who was intent on doing things his own sweet way.

But, Taylor did have to concede, Holland did have a point. There was no actual evidence or Intel to justify kicking down Morgan's door – and whatever might be generally believed, the cops were usually very careful before entering someone's home without permission or a warrant.

It didn't stop Taylor from thinking that Vickers was in the house, but the strategy was now to keep the premises under surveillance and wait for Jimmy to pop out or pop in.

Which is how Taylor found himself sitting alongside Addison in a street about a mile from Morgan's house … waiting.

And increasingly, Taylor was becoming more irritated by Addison, who stuffed a pair of earbuds in and listened to his iPod.

At ten that morning, four hours into their tour, they were given permission to take a break, get something to eat.

Time for some nosh. Taylor yanked out Addison's earbuds.

***

On the face of it, it looked as though the cops had given up watching Morgan's house. At least the obvious ones who'd been easy to spot had vanished. But Jimmy wasn't going to be taken in by that. He knew they would still be there, but now more discreet and he had pinpointed the ones still keeping her house under surveillance. It had taken time and patience, but eventually he was sure of their location.

The first was a watcher sitting in the darkness of the front bedroom in the house opposite. Jimmy knew who lived there, an old lady by herself, and it would have been easy for the cops to manipulate her into using the room.

Jimmy thought the guy was doing a good job. He rarely moved, but sat in the gloom at the back of the room and his position, all credit to him, was only compromised when the old lady entered the room with a cup of tea for him.

Jimmy smiled, remembering something similar happening to him once, many months ago near Lashkar Gah. He had found an OP in a house in a friendly village and he and his unit were watching and waiting for a Taliban soldier to set up an IED on the road into the village, a route used often by British forces. Their position had been revealed by an over-friendly resident bringing them food and tea.

That day had been a complete fuck-up.

Sometimes, the local friendlies were often as dangerous as the enemy.

It had taken Jimmy an hour to spot the guy and he was sure he was the only one watching the front of Morgan's house.

Any comings or goings that way would be spotted and reported.

So leaving by the front was a no-no.

At the back, Morgan had a small garden, surrounded by a six foot high panelled fence. She also had a shed, and a there was a narrow gap on each side of the house, maybe eight feet wide, with a fence in the middle, dividing her property from the ones either side.

Beyond the back fence was a brick built terraced row. The end property of this was a convenience store, but the remainder of the row had been divided into flats, ground and first floor, the occupants of which remained fairly static. But there was one first floor flat in the middle of the terrace that had housed many residents over the years and was also often vacant.

As it was that morning.

But when Jimmy had turned up at Morgan's house the night before and had been keeping an eye out for anything that would warn him of the presence of a watcher, he had noticed that the back bedroom window of that particular flat did not have a curtain at it.

Now, the morning after, a curtain had mysteriously appeared.

He knew that was where they were watching the back of the house from.

By evaluating the angles, he worked out that they could clearly see the patio door of Morgan's property, but because of the position of the shed in her garden, it would only be possible to see the top of the back door, but not the rest of it and anyone who stepped out could not be seen until they walked into the garden, the shed covering their exit.

A blind spot.

A fucking big blind spot, Jimmy thought – and his only way out.

Once he'd spotted this OP, he spent a further twenty minutes checking to see if there were others.

He was satisfied there were none.

Morgan handed him a coffee. 'Well?'

'Front and back. No way out of the front, but I can use the shed for cover at the back and because of the angle they're watching at, I can slide over next door's fence, keep low by their fencing, do a few more garden hops and I'm away.'

Morgan sighed, but nodded.

Jimmy told her, 'You need to go out of the back door and walk into the garden. Put something into the bin. From where they are, they can see if the back door opens, but if they don't see anyone appear they'll get sus and call it in. If they see you, it should satisfy them.'

'Should?'

'Who knows?' Jimmy said realistically. 'This ain't rocket science.'

'What about the other cops further away? Surely there'll be more, a cordon of some sort?'

'If I keep my eyes open, I'll be fine,' Jimmy said, grinning. He took a sip of the coffee, which tasted good.

'Jimmy…' Morgan said.

'I know … I know…'

***

The shop was three miles away, well beyond the perimeter cordon of the other cops watching Morgan's house. Jimmy entered it, now feeling relatively, but not completely, safe. He needed to get a few supplies, so with the peak of his baseball cap pulled low over his eyes and himself hunched down into his jacket, he moved down the aisles.

He grabbed a bottle of chilled water from the fridge display, then walked to the shelves where there was a small range of medical supplies, taking some bandages, plasters and antiseptic cream. He was planning on redressing his knife wound.

The tester came when, as he walked back towards the till with his items balanced in the crook of his arm, two uniformed cops sauntered into the shop, their hats in their hands, chatting amicably between themselves. Jimmy instantly recognised one who had knocked on Morgan's door yesterday.

He didn't know the name of either cop – but they were PCs Taylor and Addison, stood down from the OP just a few minutes earlier, on their way to the nick for a scran break, buying something on their way.

Taylor peeled off to the cold drink fridge. Addison sauntered over to the magazine rack, his eyes rising to the top shelf.

It would have been ridiculous for Jimmy to drop his goods and run.

Instead, he held his nerve.

He stepped into the gap between the officers, keeping his back to them as best he could, but although PC Taylor was looking at drinks, he also had one eye on Jimmy. Not initially because he thought the guy was the one they were after, but like all good cops, he was suspicious of virtually everyone and in particular people in shops with their hat peaks pulled down to obscure their faces.

Taylor turned slightly, keeping Jimmy in view. Watching him pay for his goods, then leave the shop.

It was only as Jimmy exited, turned right and gave Taylor a fleeting glimpse of his profile, did the young cop gasp.

He reached for his radio and called it in.

***

DCI Spencer Holland leaned back in his office chair, his face a mask of frustration. He had been completing the murder policy book, the basic narrative that all senior investigating officers were obliged to keep – in essence a running log of the murders they were in charge of.

Holland was now keeping two such journals, although he was one hundred per cent certain that the cases – Warren Evans, incinerated in his car, Danny Cross made to swallow cement and die what must have been an agonising death – were connected by one killer.

The old maxim, 'Find out how a man lived and you will find out how and why he died' was never truer in these cases. And the motive of the offender was revenge, the urge to kill someone for a wrong done or perceived to be done. And, he also thought, the killer was getting a thrill out of it.

Holland was piecing it together quickly now.

Which was good, because he also knew that cracking these could be just the final kick up the arse his career needed. Maybe this would jettison him up to the rank of superintendent three years ahead of schedule.

He had doodled on a pad, 'Location, Offender, Victim' and then the words and symbols, 'Why + When + Where + How = Who.'

'So very fuckin' true,' he said to himself, sucking his badly chewed pen.

A short, stocky detective constable called Peters swung excitedly into Holland's office. 'Guv … they think they've spotted your man.'

***

Spencer Holland hadn't moved so fast since winning the four hundred metres running race at Hendon Police Training School more than fifteen years before on his initial training. He snatched up his coat, radio, mobile phone, and legged it.

As he rushed through the low, concrete roofed police car park, he was talking urgently to comms on his mobile phone.

'And under no circumstances are they to approach him. Just maintain eyeball … yeah, I'm on my way. I want the helicopter up and I want a SWAT team … what? I know they don't fuckin' call them that. Just get it done, you know what I mean.'

He clicked the remote locking for his car, got in, fired it up and slammed it into gear.

The wheels made a satisfying squealing noise as he accelerated along the shiny concrete surface, bouncing and almost tearing off the sump as he gunned the car over the speed-calming bumps.

**

Jimmy was walking quickly, a wry grin on his face as he castigated himself for such a basic error.

Almost running face-to-face into two cops was not ideal.

But, he thought, shit happens.

How you deal with it is what counts.

He turned into the next alleyway – and it happened again.

He had to hand it to these guys. They were breathless and had worked hard to out-think him and his possible route.

PC's Taylor and Addison stood in front of him in the alley.

Taylor caught his breath. 'Alright, mate?'

Jimmy nodded.

'Got any ID on you?'

Jimmy took a pace back, hoping he wouldn't have to mix it with these guys, but he would if forced. They didn't deserve to meet him. He shook his head, kept his distance. If he could flee, that is what he would do.

Suddenly a Mercedes G-Wagon screeched around the corner and into the alley. Two men piled out, straight into the cops without hesitation. Taken completely by surprise, the young lads did their best.

But the two men, while not big guys, were hard and wiry and expertly trained to put others down quickly and efficiently.

Cops are not trained that way and they had no chance.

There was a series of well-aimed, brutally hard punches, and the cops fell.

The men then turned to Jimmy, moving towards him with purpose.

And as good as Jimmy was, he knew instinctively that these two, together, were more than a match for him. He could probably take one but while doing that the other would take him and it would be very messy.

Jimmy recognised them for what they were – military trained fighters, probably from the regiment. SAS. He also recognised them as the two guys who had been watching him in the café a couple of days before, the ones he had nailed as being out of place. They had clearly learned their lesson, realised they'd been seen and disappeared into the background. Jimmy hadn't seen them since – until now. So they were good.

Because of this, Jimmy had only one option.

He snatched the Sig out of the waistband of his pants and dropped into a combat stance. However, as quick as he was, they matched his speed and suddenly their weapons were in their hands and were pointed at Jimmy.

They stood off.

Jimmy's aim flickered from one to the other, working the angles, the speed he would need, which one to take down first, which was the weaker of the two, the slower – then put down the better, faster one, first.

From the back door of the Mercedes a huge man stepped out and Jimmy's jaw sagged as he recognised him and the man said, 'Put the gun down, Vickers.'

***

Though driving furiously through the traffic, not holding back with his shouts and 'dickhead' gestures at other drivers, and wishing he'd had that blue light fitted behind the radiator grille when he'd had the chance, it still took Spencer Holland twenty minutes to get to the scene.

He screeched to an impressive halt to see PCs Taylor and Addison sitting opposite each other in the alley like reversed bookends, while a paramedic from the ambulance called to the incident treated them.

Both young men had just been revived from unconsciousness and both had bloody noses and mouths. They would need hospital treatment.

Holland stormed up to them with anticipation, but slowed his approach as he took it all in.

The officers were hurting too much to look sheepish or embarrassed at being battered and bettered and losing a prisoner.

Holland's face screwed up with disgust. 'Dickheads,' he snarled furiously.

++++

THIRTEEN

They were in the Mercedes. Jimmy was in the back and the two guys who had laid out the cops were in front, one driving. They were cruising through the streets of London, Jimmy glowering sullenly through the smoked glass window, seeing the Thames away to his left as they travelled towards the city.

He hardly dared look at the man beside him, was cowed – maybe ashamed – to be in his presence. These were the sort of reactions that Jimmy only ever felt in this man's company, the man who had trained and mentored him, moulded him into the man that he had become. Carved him from a snotty-nosed kid into a one-man killing machine and everything that went with that.

And now, perhaps, Jimmy thought he had let him down – but he knew he had to fight against this man's influence for the first time in his life.

'Didn't expect to see you, Colonel,' Jimmy mumbled. 'You here to take me back?'

He had said the words, asked the question, without looking at him.

Now he turned his head slowly.

Colonel Leach shook his head. 'The sooner you report in, son, the better this can be for everyone involved.'

'Everyone will have to wait.'

The Colonel's voice dropped low and became a growl. 'This ain't optional, James.' The use of the name 'James' made Jimmy shudder. Few people ever called him that. His mother and father when they were angry or annoyed with him. Morgan at certain times, under certain conditions. Basically the people he loved or who loved him were the ones who used 'James.' And that fact made him wonder what the hell his relationship with Leach truly was. Jimmy was as sure as he could be that there wasn't love behind it. But over the years it had become almost too complex to disentangle and analyse. And yet, in return, Jimmy only ever called the man sitting by him by his rank and surname, or 'sir' – and Jimmy never used the accolade 'sir' with anyone else.

Leach went on. 'Fact remains, you are a serving soldier in the most elite force on this plant. And Rooker knows the Afghan spilled his guts to you and he wants what you know.'

That was another name – person – to conjure with: Rooker. Hearing it jarred Jimmy, but it didn't alter anything.

'Got some things to finish off and then I'll come in.'

Leach leaned back thoughtfully, staring through Jimmy as he said, 'This isn't going to bring 'em back son, what you're doing. Now you're a good lad and a hell of a good soldier – the best – but you gotta let this go before it turns into a shit storm even I can't clear up.'

His words were convincing and Jimmy heard them and knew them to be true. Jimmy held firm. It would have been so easy to relent. 'I'll stop when they're down,' he stated. He regarded Leach, letting the man know for certain he meant what he said, even though it made him nervous because he was defying him. 'Then I'm out.'

'Out?'

'Seen enough blood for a lifetime. Want a normal life. It's on offer now and I don't want to fuck it up.'

Leach continued to look through Jimmy. 'Normal? What is normal, James Vickers? Cushy job and desk over in Whitehall? Maybe drive a forklift around a grubby warehouse, stacking pallets? Newspaper and sandwiches on your half-hour lunch break, flask of grey coffee? People like you,' – here Leach's eyes came into focus on Jimmy – 'are beyond social integration. They sit here.' He held out his right hand flat, palm down, parallel to the ground. 'And you sit here.' He raised his hand a foot upwards to a new level. 'You sit here, psychologically tweaked to be superior to all these drones walking the streets.' He paused for effect, mesmerising Jimmy, and although his next words were clichéd, they revealed a fundamental truth. 'A lion walking amongst lambs.'

He looked back out of the window and continued, his voice lulling Jimmy, with its baritone and rhetoric, as it had done for so many years. He was like the Pied Piper and Jimmy was a kid from Hamelin. 'These people, if they knew what you've done to keep them living their mundane lives, they'd kneel and kiss your feet.'

Jimmy sat back, breathed deeply, inhaling all this, fighting his conditioned urge, desperate not to fall under Leach's spell.

It was hard when Leach said, 'You are a hero, son.'

'You realise that if they hadn't locked me up, I would've been here for them? I was due home on leave the day before they were killed.'

Leach sighed, realised that Jimmy was on a collision course that he was unable to derail.

'And I was the one who left the prison door open,' Leach said.

'I know,' Jimmy said.

The two men looked at each other, then Leach said to the driver, 'Pull over.' As the Mercedes stopped, Leach said to Jimmy, 'You've got forty-eight hours to get your personal shit wrapped up and then this passes over to Rooker ... and he is not the pussycat I am.'

***

'Watch and shoot.'

The firing range commander, a sergeant from the firearms training unit, stood four paces behind the officer standing on the start line of the thirty metre range. In his hand he had a wireless remote control, and with it he was able to control everything that was about to happen down the range – with the exception of the human being who was about to be tested.

The firearms officer stood ready and relaxed, flexing his fingers. He had his ear defenders in place – as did every other person in the range – and his safety glasses on. He was not in his full firearms kit as this was just a basic training walk down the range.

He was armed with the Glock 17 pistol with a seventeen round magazine, the standard issue firearm for officers on the Metropolitan Police branch known as SCO19. This exercise, which would probably last not much more than a minute, was simply one of a number that this particular unit – the Specialist Firearms Officers, or SFO's – would run through that day, and there was little room for error. Every single one of them was required to have a 90% accuracy rate on all shoots, not just an average, and if this target was not met, their firearms authorisation would be revoked immediately.

These were officers, though, who were so good that if they didn't get at least 95% on each shoot, they would suffer a lot of grief from their team members.

The range itself was kitted out with various obstacles which could either be seen as cover or hazards, such as low walls (made of hardboard), stacks of tyres, a large white fridge/freezer and other bits of debris that also included a pair of legs from a dress shop dummy that stuck out from behind a wall at the end of the range. Victim or villain?

The officers would not know until they reached it and saw whether or not the dummy had been armed with a submachine gun or was carrying a baby.

At the very far end of the range were the targets and they were varied. All were life-size. Some were the standard 'charging soldier' targets that flipped head on, then flipped back. Others were moving targets that, like a fairground shooting range, skimmed back and forth across the range, either slowly or quickly, depending on how the training sergeant had set up the timings.

But not every target was an actual 'target'.

Some were clearly hostiles: men with guns, men holding hostages … women holding hostages.

Some were innocents – such as the hostages themselves or a woman holding a child (who might be armed) which on first glance could look like a hostage situation, but wasn't.

The SFOs had to make those instant decisions. They had to assess what they saw, analyse it, then make the decision. Shoot or not.

Many an innocent vicar had been shot dead in this situation. And many a would-be firearms officer had lost their 'ticket' because they'd killed a baby, albeit a cardboard one.

So a basic walk down the range wasn't just a bit of target practice, and although there was nothing else to deal with other than what appeared, it was very stressful. It was a test of reaction, being able to read a situation, do what was right and justified within milliseconds. And to add to the psychology and difficulty of this, there was background noise, delivered by a surround sound hi-fi system, which was a mix of demonstrating crowd noises, traffic – including trains – and, of course, the usual accompaniment for the jobs on which these officers were deployed – rap music.

All played out under averagely poor lighting conditions.

This was one of the easier exercises.

The background sound came on, a pounding drum and bass line.

'Walk,' the instructor told the officer.

He began to move slowly forward.

And thirty metres away, the first target flicked into view.

The officer reacted, his hand going to his pistol, and he went down for cover behind a low wall. But he did not draw the gun. It was the bloody woman and a baby.

She appeared for two seconds, was gone.

The officer started to rise and as he did, another target appeared. This time it was youth pointing a gun.

The officer came out and double tapped. Bang, bang. Two rounds almost simultaneously.

The target disappeared.

The booming beat filled the range.

Maybe a minute later the walk was done. Half way through, the officer had reloaded a full magazine under cover, and reached the target line. The range lights came up, the music turned off and the officer breathed as he slid out the empty magazine, slid back the rack and showed the instructor that his weapon was empty and safe.

'Clear,' he said.

'Clear,' the instructor confirmed.

After a short conversation between the two men – the instructor had noticed one or two points that could be worked on, mainly in connection with the grip – the shoot was then scored. Ninety-eight per cent.

'But it could be significantly better,' the instructor said.

'That's what my golf pro told me,' the officer laughed, re-holstering the Glock and walking back down the range where the other members of this particular SFO team had been observing the shoot.

They jeered. He expected nothing more than derision. Nothing was ever good enough for these twats, but he loved each and every one of them – and would, if necessary, lay down his life for them as he knew they would for him. That's how close the SFOs were, a team that relied one hundred per cent on each other.

They were used for pre-planned, intelligence-led operations such as actions against armed robbers or raids on drug warehouses and could be called on to storm buildings, planes and docked boats.

Or to capture a wanted man, believed to be armed and highly dangerous.

The officer who had just walked the range was Sergeant Joe Windsor. He was a man who could instinctively lead others, who would follow without question because they knew he could be trusted. He had a great reputation for thorough planning, good briefing skills, great decision making, was known to be tough, but was also very modest and quiet and had a military background of distinction.

He shared a crack with his team until he raised his eyes and saw someone he knew hovering at the back of the range.

Tony Griffin.

Griff caught Joe's eye. They knew each other well and had briefly been colleagues at the same nick until Joe followed his career route into firearms.

Puzzled to see Griff, Joe broke away from the team.

'Hey, Griff, mate, what're you doing in this neck of the woods?'

They shook hands. 'Got a sec?' Griff asked.

'Yeah course, mate … look, walk with me, eh? We're taking a coffee break and I want to dump some stuff into my locker first.'

'Cheers.'

It was the kind of response Griff had expected from Joe, who had time for everyone.

Joe led him out of the range and into the locker room, where the rest of the team were also putting gear into lockers, chatting and fooling around.

Griff said, 'Private conversation?'

Joe opened his locker and tossed his stuff inside, said, 'Sure,' then took Griff aside to another area where they could talk quietly and not be overheard.

Griff's face was tight with doubt. Joe saw this and said, 'Spit it out, mate.'

'You know Jimmy Vickers, don't ya?'

'Yeah … ran a support op for him at FOB Robinson in Helmand about five years ago.'

'Holland closing in on him?'

'Only a matter of time.' Joe confirmed. 'Gone psycho, ain't he?'

'You know what happened to his parents, though?'

'Yeah, but that don't give him the right to go round offin' people.'

'You gotta give me the heads up if Holland finds him.' It was a hard request for Griff to make.

Joe frowned, working this out. 'You helping him?' he asked cautiously.

Griff's lips stayed rigid, but he wasn't someone who could mask the truth. He was easy to read.

'Griff, bruv! What you doin?' Joe's voice was strained with disappointment.

'I've known him since I was six, mate,' Griff started to explain, to plead, but Joe cut across him.

'It don't matter, Griff. He's out of control. If we get the order to drop him, we drop him.'

'What? And Holland isn't out of control? He don't give a fuck about anything. All he wants to do is lynch Jimmy. It'll shortcut his way to the top. Can you imagine a prick like that as a superintendent?'

The two men eyed each other.

Griff said, 'Just keep me in the loop. Please. All I ask.'

Griff patted Joe's shoulder and left. Joe watched him, now deep in troubled thought because he knew the chances were that if Jimmy Vickers didn't get caught by some other means, the likelihood would be that he'd come face to face with an SFO team – with Joe Windsor leading the assault.

And Joe Windsor was as much a professional as Jimmy Vickers.

Which meant that Joe Windsor would do his job – even if the prospect of coming up against Vickers scared the living crap out of him.

++++

FOURTEEN

But another man who was actually relishing the prospect of a confrontation with James Vickers was DCI Spencer Holland who at that moment was sitting in a nice little restaurant in Greenwich, his mind churning with how best to track the bastard down, while not understanding why information on Vickers was very, very hard to come by.

He had begun to wonder if Vickers was a spy, even. Some sort of 007 spook, possibly.

But that was only a passing thought. As far as Holland was concerned, Jimmy Vickers was nothing more than a well-trained squaddie, although the military authorities had only given him two facts – his army number and yes, that he was a serving officer.

And fucking nothing else. What?

'Cunts,' Holland muttered under his breath. If that was the way they wanted to play it, then so be it. He would find Jimmy Vickers and take him down with or without their help.

If Vickers didn't get his head blown off when he got cornered by the SFO team, Holland would take great delight in putting him through the slow grind of the criminal justice system. It would be one of the most high profile criminal trials ever, Holland promised himself. And he, Spencer Holland, cop in charge of one of the most demanding murder investigations ever in the Met, would be the man at the helm. He would revel in making the military look like a bunch of unhelpful arseholes and yet paint himself as the dogged, professional detective who had to surmount almost impossible odds to bring a multiple killer to justice.

Jimmy Vickers would get handed two life sentences and spend the rest of his pointless life rotting in Wandsworth or Dartmoor or maybe Ashworth High Security Hospital where he could cuddle up with Ian Brady. Whatever, he would eventually die in a prison hospital, probably from Aids.

Holland was sitting alone, rotating his phone in his fingers, and his mind came back to the Ministry of Defence. Whether they chose to help or not, he wasn't going to let it lie. He would continue knocking on their door, and to that end he had put in a request to see the Commissioner of the Metropolitan Police to register a formal complaint against the MoD.

Not that he was convinced it would go anywhere.

He just wanted to make the point: don't take on Spencer Holland, he's a terrier.

'Cunts,' he said again.

'I'm sorry?'

Holland, so wrapped up in his thoughts, hadn't seen the arrival of the waitress.

'Oh, I'm sorry,' he apologised, smiling charmingly. When he had to turn it on, he could be as smarmy as anyone. 'Did I really say that?'

'Yes, you did,' she said, but was not offended. She reached for his empty plate. 'Can I get you anything else?'

He shook his head and fished his credit card out of his wallet, which he handed to her. 'Just the bill, please. I gotta dash.'

'Got a murderer to catch,' he thought, but didn't say.

The waitress turned away as a woman walked past his table. She and Holland looked at each other: recognition. This was a woman who was the same age as he, blonde, stunning looking with well-trimmed bobbed hair, wearing a tight knee length suit that accentuated the fine shape of her hips and thighs and the length of her legs. She stopped abruptly as she spotted Holland and tried to give the impression this was a chance meeting of old mates. Which it wasn't. The two were old contemporaries, had been to university together, but that was as far as their relationship went.

Her name was Julia Greaves.

She was very attractive, although Holland who considered himself a ladies' man had never fancied her because she was far too cocky and assertive for his tastes. She was also his intellectual better. What Holland preferred were submissive women who knew their place – like the kitchen and the bedroom.

Even worse for Holland, she had become a journalist and now worked for one of London's top evening newspapers.

As his eyes locked into hers, his heart literally missed a beat and suddenly the fine lunch he'd just eaten tasted sour in his mouth and heavy on his belly. Heartburn was only a matter of time.

'Well I never,' Julia said, keeping up the pretence of this just being an accident. 'If it isn't Spencer Holland.'

'Julia Greaves,' Holland said glumly. He could recognise a set-up from a mile away. He wondered how she knew he'd be here. Stalking? Or just an innocent sounding phone call to the office and an unguarded word from his secretary – whose head would roll if that was the case.

Julia moved across to him. Holland thought she had the look of a lioness hunting a wildebeest. Her amber eyes narrowed briefly. Holland was on his guard.

He'd had a few minor skirmishes with her in the past and he knew she could be a pain in the arse of epic proportions to the cops because she was a ruthless digger, always on the lookout for a breaking story to which she could attach her by-line. She had done untold damage with the Stockwell shooting when armed Met cops gunned down a guy who turned out to be an innocent Brazilian called Jean Charles de Menezes, mistakenly identified as a terrorist on the way to cause death and destruction. He'd been shot seven times.

It had been a monumental cock-up, sure, but people like Greaves made it a hundred times worse than it really was, Holland thought. He was also infuriated by the irony of the remonstrations from the Brazilian government, saying that British cops were out of control. Not like in Brazil, eh, Holland had thought, where cop death squads murdered people daily. Just because they could. Fucking hypocrites.

Julia Greaves, therefore, was one to beware of, although Holland did have some sneaking admiration for her tenacity and brazen "in your fucking face-ness". She was the last person he needed to see.

Uninvited and brash, she sat down across from him.

'Two courses for lunch? Bit swish, innit? Thought you cops were fish and chips types, eat on the go, crooks to catch and all that?'

'I'm in a rush, Julia … so…' He made an apologetic gesture. The waitress returned with Holland's credit card and the wireless handset. Holland tapped in his PIN and waited for his receipt to print out.

'A rush eh? Oh yeah, you would be. Got your hands full with those two murders.'

The waitress looked sharply at her.

Holland frowned and gave his best, 'You're absurd' smile. 'Murders? I don't know what you're talking about.'

The waitress tore off the receipt and handed back to him with a 'rather you than me' look for him. She left.

Julia fixed him with her lioness eyes, her lips twisted with a cynical, confident smile.

'Spence, you are just so full of shit. Everyone knows about your killer. Three left, I heard – or at least that's the media rumour. Ask me, sounds like a vigilante ... maybe the first this century. Big, BIG story.'

Holland lowered his voice, half wondering what a wildebeest felt like when the lioness sank its fangs into its neck and started choking it. A bit like he felt right now, he guessed. 'You fuckin' run any of this and I'll end you.'

'Oh yeah?' she sneered.

'Yeah!'

The little schoolyard standoff came to an abrupt end.

Julia softened, as much as it was possible for her to do so. She went into 'cajole' mode. 'Come on, Spence, don't be a prick. People have a right to know what's going on on their streets.'

'A right to know? Really? You honestly gonna lay that one on me?'

'You know who he is, don't you?' she slid in a low-bowl. She reached across and picked up a piece of uneaten bread from the basket.

'And how would you know that?' he blustered, trying to remain calm and apparently, doing a shit job of it.

Julia giggled, recalling he had never once bettered her in a discussion or argument, even back at university. His problem was that his blue touch paper could be easily lit. He was a brittle man with little patience or, to some degree, guile. With Spencer Holland you got what you saw. That didn't mean to say he was unintelligent. He was simply a livewire, always pushing, always edgy. Whereas she sat back, thought things through – then pounced.

Lioness, Holland thought again.

'You're so shit at this. You just can't lie, Spence. It's all over your face. Look,' she leaned forward encouragingly, 'my editor will hump my leg if I bring him this. I'll show the cops in a good light...y'know...something like,' – she raised her eyes and used her hands to demonstrate what the words might look like on a billboard – '"Police say zero tolerance on Vigilante attacks. DCI Spencer Holland closing in on psycho." How about that?' She smiled playfully. 'Your name up in lights.' She almost batted her eyelashes at him, but didn't want to push it too far and send him the wrong message. The prospect of any physical contact with him truly nauseated her, though she guessed the same applied in the opposite direction. If they got together it would like two Van de Graaff generators fucking: sparks would fly, but not passionate ones.

That said, she thought she had him hooked, that her rhetoric had worked.

It hadn't.

Holland stood up to leave. 'Try the salad,' he said cruelly. 'You've put on weight since last time.'

'Look who's talking,' she quipped back childishly, knowing she'd lost.

'Great seeing you again.' Then he was gone, and Julia didn't even turn to watch him go. Instead, she reached for the glass of red wine he had been drinking and sank the residue.

'Yeah, let's do it again soon … dickhead.' She wiped her lips.

***

They decided to keep their heads down and keep apart for the time being until the danger had passed.

Now essentially leaderless, Rob and Leon found themselves without any focus in their lives, and also terrified of setting foot onto the streets in case they too met their deaths in a particularly brutal, sickening way. The fate of Warren and Danny had spooked two young men who usually walked tall and tough in their neighbourhoods. They were the ones who usually terrified others with casual beatings and shows of strength. Normally, they were afraid of no one.

Now they were terrified by their own shadows – and because they had done so many bad things in their short lives, they simply could not connect the dots.

Yes, they were under attack.

But from whom and why?

They struggled to work it out.

Initially, they'd been convinced that Caleb had taken out Warren simply because the two of them, although partners, could never see eye to eye and were always squabbling and bickering over shit. They hated each other, but they had a good profitable business going.

But Caleb had vehemently denied it when they had burst into his flat and his half-naked girlfriend had seen them off with a shotgun and her tits pointed at their heads.

Then, of course, Danny had simply disappeared after going to the toilet in The Wolf which, incidentally, was the pub where they had first latched onto George Vickers as a possible mark and followed him for weeks after discovering he worked at Cash4Gold. All the little bastard Danny had done was go to the toilet – and now he was dead.

Neither Leon nor Rob knew how he had really died. All they'd heard was that he'd been murdered. Rumours abounded in the 'hood of course. That he'd had his entrails cut out of his belly and been strangled with them; that he'd had his dick and balls cut off with a pair of secateurs and stuffed into his mouth; or that he'd had a sharpened broom handle inserted right up his arsehole, all the way through his intestines and up through his throat. Then he'd had his eyes gouged out and had ritualistic pagan markings scarred into his chest with a knife.

A killer worse than Jack the Ripper was back, haunting the streets of east London.

But then there was the phone call that Rob had made to Danny to find out just where the hell he'd gone, and the guy – the killer – had answered the phone.

Rob had only really half-taken in the shit he'd said about the old couple, even though he had been trying to concentrate, because Rob himself was half-stoned and drunk when he was speaking to the guy. It was only later did he really force himself remember the conversation, then discuss it with Leon.

'It's that fuckin' couple we did, that's what this is about,' Rob declared.

'That cunt who offed Josh with the bat?' Leon asked.

'Yeah, yeah, that's what this is about. It's fuckin' revenge.'

'Or bullshit,' Leon said. 'Someone trying to put the shits up us.'

'Yeah…whatever, Bruv. But he's offed Warren and Danny and that makes me think one thing, man…' Rob let the words hang profoundly in the air.

'We're next. Shit. So what do we do? Go to the cops?'

Rob regarded Leon as though he was insane. 'And say what? We murdered and killed an old couple, raped the shit out of the wife and set fire to 'em? And by the way, someone's pissed off at us for doing it?' It was at that point that Rob rapped Leon on the skull with his knuckles. Hard. 'Fuckin' numb twat. No, we stay low, keep apart and watch our fuckin' backs. This'll go away, man, it will. We just need to keep solid, man.'

They clashed knuckles.

Leon wasn't the brightest of the crew and the only place he could think of to get some solid sleep was by returning home to the council house where his mother lived with a succession of shithead boyfriends. They were guys who either beat him up for sport (encouraged by his mum) or who he beat up (also encouraged by his mum). Her allegiance shifted depending on circumstance. He also had a younger sister whom he hated with a vengeance. The thing about people like Leon was that, as much as they espoused their disdain and hatred for their roots and bragged about how they were gonna get out of this shit life and live one with fancy cars, shit hot women and money, it rarely happened. People like Leon were doomed from birth, but even so, when things went badly, they usually skulked home.

Which is what Leon did – and walked right into a shit storm.

Literally.

When he put his head around the back door he found his mother in the foetal position, sobbing her heart out, having just endured another beating from her present beau. He was a big, brooding ogre of a man who was sitting shovelling a Chinese takeaway into his mouth at the kitchen table, a beer can in hand.

Leon's first instinct, despite everything, was to protect his mother, even though she had given him one of the worst upbringings a kid could have.

But the boyfriend stood up, towering darkly over Leon, between him and his mother.

'Get the fuck outta here,' Leon was warned.

Leon knew he was no physical match for the guy. If he'd had a shooter or a blade he would have taken him there and then, but he backed off, much to the sneering derision of the boyfriend, and slinked upstairs where he found his sister bawling her eyes out.

'Fuck,' Leon said, exasperated. He went into his room, a box room with a camp bed. He wedged the door closed and climbed on the bed – and slept.

It was a good, four hour rest and when he awoke it was dark outside.

He stumbled downstairs and found his mother sitting in her boyfriend's lap with her hand down his boxers, jerking him off as happy as anything, while he played with her tits. This was despite her lips looking like an exploded inner tube and a huge, purple, swollen black eye and busted nose.

The man regarded Leon with evil eyes and a challenging expression as he pulled down the front of his shorts to show him exactly what was going on underneath.

Leon knew he had to get out, despite the dangers of the streets and though he was revolted by the sight of the man's mammoth cock in his mother's hand, he felt he had a similar need himself.

He stepped out into the night, keeping to the shadows, completely unaware of the dark figure of Jimmy Vickers following him with intent to kill.

++++

FIFTEEN

Leon hit the strip joint early. It was probably the sleaziest establishment of its sort in Whitechapel, occupying a basement below a row of tatty shops that included a tattoo parlour and fast food joints and was one of the few places like this that still existed in London, although this was no accolade.

It was a true dive in the real sense of the word. The girls could be paid for and taken to private booths hardly bigger than a phone box to fuck the customers any which way; or the girls who danced for the punters could very easily be encouraged, by the flash of cash, to go down on them where they sat and would provide a condom, included in the price.

The cost wasn't extravagant.

This suited Leon. Although he lived a lifestyle many of his contemporaries were jealous of, being a foot soldier for a major drug dealer, being a gangster almost, truth was he didn't have a lot of cash to go with it. He would have been better off stacking shelves in Asda, but that would have meant responsibility and turning up for work, things which Leon abhorred. Now, with Warren dead and gone, it looked as though Leon's life was about to go downhill fast. He hoped to tag into one of Warren's rival gangs, but there'd been so much bad blood between them he was doubtful about that ever happening. He thought of starting his own patch, but that move was fraught with danger and he wasn't sure if he had the necessary presence and acumen to pull it off. He guessed his best course of action would be to smooth up to Caleb and see what happened from there.

In the meantime, he had to avoid being offed and, if possible, satisfy some of his more basic urges.

It was early and the club was quiet, only a few punters at the bar or sitting around the stage watching a bored looking oldish pole dancer who had seen much better days. Leon sat low in a booth at the edge of the bar, watching the action with a pint and a vodka shot.

A slim but big breasted dancer snaked her way over and began to gyrate in front of him, wearing only a thong that left nothing to the imagination. Leon was quickly mesmerised by her boobs and shaved pubes, through which the thong travelled like a railway line through a cutting.

Leon reached out to touch, feeling his groin shift as the blood rushed to his penis.

She smacked away his hand but stood provocatively in front of him, then leaned over as he slouched down and let her breasts hang just above his face. She whispered, 'Fifty quid, blow job.' From somewhere, a condom appeared and she placed the silver foil packet between her teeth, shaking it.

Leon gasped, 'Okay,' and managed to reach for the cash in his jeans pocket and stuff it into her greedy hand. The money disappeared with the same trickery as the condom had appeared. She continued to move to the throbbing music, skilfully unfastening his flies and pulling down the front of his boxers.

She tore open the condom packet and extracted the latex sheath with her teeth and eased it over Leon's cock. Her head went down into his lap and she worked him slowly, deftly, expertly. Leon started to squirm and moan.

They were interrupted by the arrival of a waitress bearing a drink on a tray. The exotic dancer continued unfazed, although she did look up sideways at her work colleague.

'Fuck do you want?' Leon said.

The waitress put the drink on the low table. 'It's from that bloke over there.' She jerked her thumb in the direction of the bar. 'Asked me to give you this, too.'

She left an A4 sized envelope next to the drink. The woman kept working on Leon, her head bobbing and weaving, but he was distracted now, trying to enjoy the blow job but puzzled by the arrival of the drink and envelope. No stranger had ever bought him a drink before and the envelope was curious.

He tried to keep hard, but the more he tried, the less easy it was. His concentration wandered and he was now looking across the pole dancing stage to the bar, trying to see someone he knew. There was only one person there now, sitting on a stool and Leon didn't know him.

He peered through the gloom and smoke – non-smoking legislation would never reach this establishment – and saw the man's face clearly for the first time, at the exact moment the pole dancer, with her back to Leon, spun away from the pole, set her feet wide apart and bent down so that Leon saw him through the varicose-veined legs and at the same time got a view of the dancer's bottom and sagging, dangling breasts.

The man at the bar raised a glass to him.

Leon pushed the dancer away from him. He had lost his erection anyway and she was gamely trying to give him his money's worth. He grabbed the envelope, tore it open and pulled out the contents.

A full colour photograph.

Showing Danny Cross, dead, with his mouth cemented open.

Leon yelped and lunged off his seat, trying to stow his penis away, zip up and yank up his jeans, at the same time snapping the condom off and throwing it away. It landed in someone's drink. He ran, barging his way through people as fear gripped him, a fear that only the next victim of a killer could feel, almost debilitating. He bolted to the rear emergency exit, feeling as though he was running through treacle, and the sign above the door of a red man running was entirely appropriate.

He smashed up the release bar, breaking the seal, and was out into a back alley, skidding to a halt, his head turning one way, then the next, desperately trying to decide which way to flee.

He went right. But it wouldn't have mattered.

Jimmy Vickers dropped casually off the stool, tossing some money on the bar. He headed for the main exit, threading his way unhurriedly between the customers and girls, stepping out onto the street.

Leon ran hard, arms pumping, everything wanting to explode, terror burning inside like he had never known, the horrific image of Danny imprinted on his brain. His friend, a guy he'd known and run with for years ... dead.

He turned, bolted along a pavement, not really caring where he was heading. All he wanted to do was put distance between himself and that fucking mad man psycho killer.

Jimmy hopped into the Toyota Hi-Lux.

He stayed even and unexcited. He'd done this before. Many times. All it took was training, patience and a touch of instinct. To think like the animal he was hunting down.

He cruised slowly, easily.

The streets were fairly quiet – advantage to him.

And then there Leon was, emerging from an alleyway, gasping for breath, doubled over, hands on knees. A young man, but nowhere near as fit as he should be. He was going to explode.

He thought he was safe now. He must have run a fucking mile. He walked on swiftly.

A hundred metres behind, Jimmy crawled close to the kerb, sidelights on.

Leon ducked into another alley, glancing both ways before pitching in, seeing no one on foot that could be the killer.

Twenty metres down he stopped in his tracks as a very peculiar sensation flitted through his whole being. His skin constricted. He turned slowly, his breath held tight in his lungs.

And he saw the wide and tall four wheel drive vehicle almost filling the width of the alley, from wall to wall.

No lights on.

Despite the pounding of the blood in his head, Leon could hear the gentle burble of the car's engine, see the dark figure of the driver at the wheel.

'Fuck this,' Leon said, then screamed, 'Come on, you cunt.'

For four seconds, nothing.

Leon's fury began to rise. 'I said, come on, come and get me.'

The car remained still and unlit.

Then every single spotlight on the bull bars, plus the normal fitted headlights, came on, bathing the alleyway in powerful white light. The engine roared and the vehicle surged forward.

It took a second for Leon to react. He spun and ran a terrifying race, the shadow of his running self ahead of him, breaking the beam of the headlights. He was running in a nightmare of twisted shadow and light and the roar of the engine sounded demonic, like the wail of a terrible beast.

He went sideways into another alley, expecting the corner to be too tight for the car, but it still came, getting closer, bearing down on him, surely going to reach him and then gore him like a bull.

He ran.

Then he could run no further.

He had gone straight into a dead end, and scratched desperately at the wall, trying to climb it, but could not. He fell back and faced the car, short of breath, his lungs clawing for air.

The car was twenty metres away, motionless. The lights blazed.

Leon was trapped.

'Come on,' he goaded weakly as he sank low, his back against the wall. Then he said, 'Oh God,' as he saw what was happening.

The man from behind the wheel was out of the car, standing in front of it, his frame silhouetted and enlarged by the blaze of the lights.

'Oh God,' Leon gulped again.

The figure came slowly towards him and Leon saw the familiar outline of a baseball bat in his left hand, hanging almost nonchalantly by his side, and the black distinctive shape of a pistol in his right hand.

The man kept coming. Suddenly the pistol had gone and the bat had transferred to his right hand. Leon whimpered and covered his head with his hands.

Jimmy Vickers stepped up and unleashed his anger upon him, beating Leon with the bat – thud, thud, thud – an assault that seemed to go on forever.

***

Leon regained consciousness. Although disorientated and in agony, he knew he was hanging upside down, the top of his shaven skull only inches above the dirty concrete floor of a deserted warehouse. His vision swam. He passed out.

Only to wake up again, but this time something was different. He was still hanging upside down, but now a tube had been inserted into his right nostril and taped securely there.

He took this in, feeling the tube somewhere down his throat, and realised other things.

His hands were taped behind his back and his legs had been taped together, so he was very tightly trussed up.

He saw a pair of feet in the periphery of his vision.

Then he realised he was moving upwards, being pulled up away from the ground like a carcass of meat, inch by inch. After the first pull, he also realised something else: his ankles had been bound together by strands of barbed wire and as he was winched up, the wire ripped into his flesh and blood streamed down his naked legs, for he was also completely naked.

He screamed an unearthly noise as he went up inch by jerking inch on a pulley wheel contraption of sorts and whoever was doing it was purposely doing it in a jerky way so the barbs cut into him.

Eventually Leon's eyes were level with the eyes of his captor and tormentor.

Jimmy Vickers looked unemotionally at Leon.

'Oh God, please mate, I'm sorry.' Leon squirmed, frantically trying to free himself, twisting and pulling, but he could hardly move and all he did was make the barbs dig deeper into the flesh and bone of his ankles. It looked like a Houdini trick gone fatally wrong. He gave up and said, 'I'm sorry.'

'What are you sorry for?'

'Whatever I did to you.'

'What?' Jimmy almost laughed. 'You don't even know, do ya?'

Jimmy pulled out his pistol and tapped the muzzle on Lean's forehead, making a dull knocking sound. 'That's the problem … little pricks running around, burning people alive, neglecting the emotional devastation of your actions.'

Leon took this in, then started to sob. 'Sorry, sorry, sorry.'

'I know mate, I know. Everyone's sorry. Sorry is fuck all. Sorry is a castaway word on the breath of the hopeful who have gone too far to right their wrongs.'

That philosophy was lost on Leon. 'Eh?'

Jimmy looked away and pointed with the gun. 'See that?'

There was a table next to Leon and the tube that had been inserted into his nose snaked out and led to a small electric pump and a further tube from that pump was connected to a hose.

'What is it?'

'I bought you a drink earlier and you didn't drink it.' Jimmy lowered Leon back down so that his skull was again just inches from the floor. He reached across and depressed a button on the pump. A harmless sounding hum kicked in and the pump began to work, drawing in water from the hose which was connected to a tap. The pump pulled the water through and pushed it out into the tube inserted into Leon's nose.

He coughed and spluttered as the water, fresh and cold, started to dribble out of his free nostril and mouth.

Jimmy switched off the pump.

Leon gasped for air as the water cascaded out from his facial orifices. Again he started to squirm and fight to free himself, causing the barbs to dig even deeper.

'It's just water,' Jimmy said. 'It's just water.'

'Please, mate,' Leon spluttered and coughed. 'Please, mate, please.'

Jimmy was unmoved. 'I'm not your enemy here, mate. Gravity is your enemy. I'll tell you why. All that water is gonna go down into your skull and the pressure is going to build up and build up. And then, because it's water, and water likes to find its own level, it's going to try and find a way out through your ears, your nose, your mouth – your eyes. Pop! Or you might just suffocate and drown first.'

Jimmy reached across, turned the pump on. The motor started to hum, the water began to draw.

Leon tried to shout, but the water was already inexorably building up. He struggled, spat, gurgled and gargled as he watched the upside down figure of Jimmy Vickers walk away from him.

++++

SIXTEEN

Spencer Holland looked around the Major Incident Room that was now up and running to deal with the two murders, Warren Evans and Danny Cross. He had a certain pride about what he had achieved in such a short space of time, because getting an MIR operating was no easy thing and to get it staffed properly was also a nightmare, but he had pulled it off.

He had, as far as possible, staffed it with people he knew and trusted, and it was structured as per the Murder Investigation Manual and Major Incident Room guidelines.

He walked around it now, looking carefully at the walls on which many flipchart sheets had been Blu-tacked. They contained information about the murders, including timelines, crime scene assessments, details about the victims and what little was known about the offender.

Holland paused as he studied the flipcharts, his eyes playing over the details and getting very fucking annoyed.

'Shit,' he said to no one in particular. He stalked back into his office and logged into the computer system and onto the force intranet. He began to search.

After half an hour he hadn't discovered anything he didn't already know. But then, as he looked at the screen, his mouth went very dry and he sat bolt upright.

'Shit,' he said again, this mine in awe of himself. 'Now that's what I call a fucking coincidence.'

He reached for his desk phone and dialled an internal number.

'DCI Holland,' he introduced himself grandly. 'I want the full physical files that we have on Warren Evans and Daniel Cross...I know I can look at them online ... I don't want to look at them online ... I want them here on my desk in front of me in ten minutes in nice Manila file covers ... do I make myself clear? I'm in charge of a double murder investigation for fuck's sake and people like you,' – he almost said "minions" – 'do as I say...understand? Ten fucking minutes.' He slammed the phone down. 'Pen pushing arsehole.'

He rocked back in his chair, almost tipping it over he went so far back.

Then his mobile phone rang. He scooped it up from his desk blotter and saw who was calling. Instantly his demeanour changed.

'Sir,' he answered as smooth as silk. It would hardly be in his best interests to insult a chief superintendent.

***

To be honest, the last thing Spencer Holland needed at that moment in his life was a pep talk from a boss. But he could hardly refuse, so twenty minutes later he was walking through a fairly swish West End restaurant to get to the bar and meet Chief Superintendent Dennis Walsh, a man who was both friend and mentor.

Walsh was late fifties, medium build, well-spoken and had a commanding presence that Holland could only dream of emulating. He seemed to own the very space he stood on and surrounded him. He was waiting for his drink to arrive when Holland sidled up next to him. Holland respected the guy, not only for his aura, but also for his suavity, something else the brash Holland could only dream of. Walsh seemed immune to the stress and strain of being a high level cop, took it all in his stride, but still dealt with people and situations with ruthless efficiency. People often came away from him not realising they had been shafted – until much later. Whereas Holland did not have that skill. He was easily riled by pressure and when he dealt with anyone, there was no subtlety about it: they knew they had been dealt with.

As would, Holland thought, the next person in my line of fire. That was one bastard who would know for sure. Unfortunately, that little encounter had to be put on hold for a little while.

'Chief Superintendent,' Holland said by way of greeting.

Walsh turned slowly. 'Ahh, Spencer … you having a drink?'

As much as he would have liked to drink a brewery dry, Holland said, 'No thank you.'

'Go on, won't hurt, on or off duty.'

'No, really sir,' Holland said, smiled politely and settled himself on the barstool alongside Walsh. 'I'm never off duty.'

Walsh grinned and ordered him a gin and tonic anyway. The drink came and Holland drowned the spirit with the mixer. He wanted to keep a clear head.

Walsh gestured for Holland to follow him and led him to a table close to the window, obviously reserved, and they sat opposite each other. Walsh said, 'Heard you've got your plate full. Some fairly gruesome murders.'

Holland shrugged as a tinge of anxiety shot through him. He thought that maybe this was going to be snatched away from him. His throat went arid and he took a generous swig of his drink, the ice clanking against his teeth. 'Nothing I can't handle,' he said confidently. 'I'll get him.'

'You think it's the same person?'

'Possibly. Would you say that's a safe assessment?'

'Lord knows.' Walsh raised his eye heavenwards, as if he should know such a thing. Walsh was presently working from New Scotland Yard on a personnel and change project on behalf of the Commissioner. It was one of those projects that seemed to have been going on for years without any result in the offing and Walsh didn't appear to want it to end. Projects had become his speciality and though they never seemed to deliver what they promised, he was highly thought of in the hierarchy, taking on many a poisoned chalice that others shied away from. He was next up for promotion and Holland envied the guy's career. Walsh went on, 'That's why me and your dad became chief supers, so we didn't have to deal with the shits any more.'

Walsh had mentioned Holland's father, who was a chief superintendent in a northern force, approaching the end of an illustrious, though mainly headquarters-based career. Walsh and his father knew each other from the many training courses they had attended. Both of them were professional course-goers. A good long course was an excellent way of networking and legitimately keeping well away from the front line.

Walsh noticed a disheartened look come into Holland's eyes.

He paused, then began, 'In 2003, I went to New York on a holiday with the missus,' – and at that point, Holland thought, 'here comes the pep' – and downed another mouthful of his G&T which was starting to taste rather nice. 'The week we were there, the bin men were on strike. No rubbish had been collected for a week. You cannot imagine the smell. A city that size – what, ten million people? I don't know. And in August, too. People don't see or really take notice of bin men or care how they toss people's rubbish, but if they don't, they know about it and cities start to reek. Do you get where I'm going with this?'

Holland's face twisted into a pompous smile. He nodded.

'Do you know who you are in this story, Spencer?'

'The guy clearing all the scum to make the streets cleaner?' he hazarded.

'Yes, you are.' Again Walsh paused for effect. He was one of the Met's best orators and he knew how to keep an audience in the palm of his hand. 'If you're an idiot.'

It was like the nick of a knife blade and Holland's pomposity burst and farted away like a balloon losing air.

Walsh leaned forward, intense. 'The cop who thinks he can clean up the streets is a deluded fool. Don't rock the boat, look after number one. Just between me and you', – here Walsh tapped his large nose – 'I'm going up very soon.' He jerked his forefinger towards the ceiling. 'And when I do there will be a vacuum and it'll need filling, if you get my drift. I've put it about, and there have been some nods of agreement from he who shall be obeyed, that when the shuffle starts you will be going upwards, too. Up and sideways and you could be the youngest superintendent in London by the end of this year, which is not far away. Nice, or what?'

Holland lapped it up. 'Oh yes, sir.'

'But you cannot leave a shit storm behind you, Spencer. That's not how it's done.' He pointed at Holland. 'Wrap up this gruesome case quick. Get your statements, get 'em scraped off the streets, and above all keep the media out of this. We can't afford any more scandal, because if the Commissioner starts to hear about shit getting out of control, he might change his mind very quickly. It's fuckin' cold on nights in Limehouse, if you get my drift, Spencer. You'll be demoted before you can say Katie Price is a virgin. You understand? This is all in the balance and if you put your weight in the right direction, then you go up on the see-saw, then jump on the climbing frame. Understand?'

Holland finished his drink. 'Yes sir,' and thought, 'Rock and a hard place.' A pep talk, a promise, a kick up the arse, a threat – all rolled into one. Nice.

'Now let's have another drink and relax.'

***

Holland's head was a mush by the time he left Walsh's company as he realised that his predicament was actually make or break. He'd thought that solving the murders would be a good step for his career, but now, reading between the lines, it was deal maker – or breaker, not something he could just shrug aside if he didn't bring it to a successful conclusion. He had to get a result fast, not allow this shit to drag on any longer. Otherwise this shit would stick.

The mention of nights in Limehouse made Holland shudder with abhorrence. His idea of a career move was to a nice corner office in Scotland Yard's Empress Building next to Earl's Court Exhibition Centre. A great view of Brompton Cemetery and Stamford Bridge (he was a keen Chelsea supporter) and the opportunity to watch planes coming in to land at Heathrow while dispensing authority to all and sundry. Not fucking Limehouse.

He had to walk to get his thoughts in some kind of order. He ended up by the Thames, near to the Houses of Parliament where steam pouring up from a hotdog stand and the resultant aroma made him realise he was excessively hungry.

He reached into his pocket for change and joined the short queue, ordered a hotdog and coffee. He took his little feast over to the condiments table and squeezed ketchup and mustard onto his sausage and added several shots of sugar into his coffee. Normally he liked his coffee black and unsweetened. Today, his energy levels were sagging and he needed a boost.

A man stepped beside him with just a coffee and said, 'After you, mate.'

Holland passed the sugar pourer over and refitted the lid on his polystyrene cup.

'Bloody cold, isn't it?' the man commented.

'Yeah, whatever,' Holland said, disinterested.

The man made eye contact with Holland, who started to grow uncomfortable – but for the wrong reasons. He assumed he was being tapped up for sex.

'Do we know each other?' he asked the man aggressively, his body language making it plain he was a raving heterosexual.

The man eased the lid onto his coffee, took a sip and said, 'My name is Colonel Leach.'

***

They stood on Victoria Embankment, looking across the Thames to the London Eye which rotated slowly, inevitably. The river looked murky brown and moved slowly, inevitably.

Leach sipped his coffee while Holland leaned casually on the wall, watching him carefully, trying to get his measure and being unsettled by his presence. Leach was a big man and came across as physically and mentally powerful. His stone-grey eyes particularly had the deadly knowing look of someone with great knowledge and experience who had seen things no man should.

But, 'Fuck that,' Holland thought. This could be the very breakthrough he needed.

He was one hundred per cent off-track, as the words Leach spoke made very clear. 'Gonna need you to hand over everything you've got on him.'

Holland's mouth creased up. 'Yeah, right, like that's gonna happen, mate. Other way round, if you please.'

'Kid belongs to us, not you.'

'Don't think so,' Holland guffawed. Then he said, 'Colonel Leach, or whoever you claim you are, he belongs to me when he's taking the law into his own hands on my patch.'

Leach walked back and forth a few times, sipping his coffee thoughtfully. Then he stopped and looked at Holland, who stared blandly at him, challenging.

'Let me explain something to you, chief inspector.'

'I'm listening,' Holland said, but his demeanour said, 'I'm listening but I'm not taking any fucking notice of this.'

'September 2009. We got Intel there was a major attack being planned on British soil. This would've made 7/7 look like a dress rehearsal. We ran an op to bring in the guy running the attack. The Taliban came down on us like piss rain. Biggest firefight I'd ever seen. There was no way we could get the prick out of there to a safe environment, so we had to get what we needed there and then.' He paused, recalling. 'Took Jimmy Vickers ten minutes alone with this guy to get him to spill his guts. While we held off thirty Taliban, he gave Vickers everything. Took the guy's life as well, just for good measure.

Cold blood. We had to let that one go. Now these people do not fear death, chief inspector, they welcome it, so you gotta ask yourself how Vickers got the goods. How do you extract information from a man who ain't afraid of dying?'

Holland remained quiet, listening, not remotely impressed.

'In the end, we were in danger of being overrun. We had to get out of there and we couldn't find Vickers ... turns up three days later at Camp Bastion, not a scratch on him. No one knows how he did it. But you need to know this, Mr Holland – if Jimmy Vickers does not want to be found, he won't be.' Leach's eyes stared hard into Holland's, reinforcing his point. 'He'll channel his emotions, he'll finish up on these guys and then he'll vanish.'

'You're fulla bullshit,' Holland uttered, breaking the moment of tension – and realising there would be no help ever from the military on this. The lack of response from them wasn't just bad admin or communication. It was deliberate. He leaned towards Leach. 'I will find him and he will be mine. It's what I do.'

For a few seconds they had a glaring contest until Leach took a threatening step forward, making Holland jump, thinking he was going to get punched.

Leach's voice was full of menace. 'You lay a finger on our boy and I will come down on you so hard they'll be using paint stripper to mop you up.'

He gave Holland once last, knowing look, then turned away.

Holland watched him and said, 'Arsehole,' under his breath. Certainly not loud enough for Leach to hear.

***

Holland was on the hunt. He checked the computerised duty states on the intranet and knew that his quarry was working that day and all he had to do was track him down. He stalked the corridors and eventually spotted PC Tony Griffin emerging from the sergeant's office, where he collared him.

'PC Griffin – with me, mate.'

He had thought of doing the, 'My Office, now,' shit, but decided against it.

***

Holland's office was actually quite pleasant, if functional. But there was no view of Chelsea FC from it. No view of anything.

He moved in ahead of Griff and motioned for him to sit while he slid in behind his desk but did not sit.

Griff's face had remained flat. Underneath, he had a very bad feeling about this encounter.

Holland gathered up the two thick Manila files sitting on top of each other on his blotter and, for effect, he dumped them back down side by side under Griff's nose with a dull thud and a whoosh of air displacement.

Griff knew exactly what they were. His throat constricted.

Holland folded his arms.

'Major coincidence, isn't it, that the last officer to access these two gentlemen's files was you? Prior to their deaths, I might add.'

Griff looked at the photographs pinned to the front of each file. Mug shots, face on, sideways, custody record numbers on boards along the bottom of each photo. Both were of sneering, defiant young men.

Warren Evans and Danny Cross. Shaven headed, tough looking boys from the streets, a starkness behind the eyes showing they didn't care what the authorities had to throw at them.

'You accessed the Intel files on both these individuals and now they are dead,' Holland reiterated. 'You also did a PNC check on a red Ford Focus that belonged to this guy,' Holland tapped his finger on Warren's photograph. 'He wasn't the registered owner, but Intel had him down as the owner and user and this was the car in which he was incinerated, while still alive, according to the PM result. You checked this number before he died.' Holland slipped a PNC print-out under Griff's nose. His collar number was on the sheet.

Griff opened his mouth to protest.

'Ah-ah-ah,' Holland stopped him and waggled a finger. 'Don't want to hear a word from you, yet.'

He then placed half a dozen black and white photographs in front of Griff, spread them out. They had been screen-printed from the CCTV footage from The Wolf pub. They showed Jimmy Vickers and his 4x4 and just one of the images caught Jimmy's features enough – maybe – to ID him. Griff certainly could.

Griff sifted through them. His heart was now slamming.

'James Vickers, soldier boy. Currently serving with what appears to be a somewhat dubious department of our Majesty's armed forces. MoD aren't exactly falling over to fill us in on him, but we understand interrogation is his speciality. And, would you believe it, they want to know immediately when we apprehend him. "Our boy" they call him. How very fucking sweet.' Holland regarded Griff stonily. 'Is he done, or are there any more?'

Griff didn't answer.

Holland leaned forwards, arms still folded. 'I need to know who's next – or do I have to send a request to the PNC Bureau and the Intelligence Unit to ask them to put up your name and ask for every search you've done in the last week? Y'know, the ones where the people you checked have, "accidentally", died. Just after you checked them?' Holland tweaked his fingers on the word accidentally.

Griff's face rose. 'You don't need to know anything. The only thing you need to do is stay out of his way.'

Holland stood bolt upright. 'I'm not staying out of anyone's way, sunshine. I'm gonna find him and I'm gonna lock him up and whoever he's after for whatever they've done.'

Griff could not hold back a sarcastic grin. 'The last thing he's gonna let you do is lock 'em up. He's gonna wipe 'em out, or die trying.'

'Die trying's good enough for me. He thinks he can go vigilante on my streets, he's got another think coming.'

'He doesn't care about you or the law. He doesn't care about justice.' Griff shook his head. 'He just wants one thing...'

Holland waited.

'Revenge,' Griff said. 'Thing is,' Griff went on, suddenly feeling the righteousness of this now, after much agonising and soul searching, 'he'll do more justice in a week than we could hope to do in a year.'

'We?' Holland gasped incredulously. 'Mr Griffin – and I say "mister" advisedly – I think it is safe to say you ceased being a police officer from the moment you started helping your little friend out.'

'Well good luck finding him, then.' Griff stood up and smiled slyly as he quoted Holland back to his face. '"Might take a while but, eh, slow justice is better than no justice. That's what I say".' He patted Holland on the side of his arm, and Holland looked down to where Griff had touched him, repulsed.

Griff left, leaving Holland seething at his own inability to intimidate.

At that moment, DC Porter swung into the office, as he had a habit of doing so.

'What?' Holland snapped.

***

'Oh my fucking shit,' Holland cursed time and again as he circled the upside down hanging body of Leon Romes. 'Oh my fucking shit.'

Uncharacteristically, Holland had donned a forensic suit that was so loose and badly fitting on his narrow frame, it billowed like the Michelin Man. But he wasn't concerned by his appearance. He was concerned that night shifts in Limehouse were getting closer and closer.

He stopped his circling and looked at the naked body, from the horrendously cut ankles, wrapped in barbed wire, the blood having run down his legs, down his thighs and all the way down his body to his neck and shoulders.

Holland bent low and inspected the tube inserted into Leon's nostril, following it with his eyes to the electric pump and beyond that to the hose pipe connected to the tap.

He also looked at Leon's eyes, which had been forced out of their sockets and hung down on their optic nerves.

Holland barely had the strength in his legs to stand upright again. He felt so weak and voraciously hungry, recalling with ire that his last food had been a hotdog on the Thames Embankment with the army spook or whatever the guy named Leach thought he was. A mysterious wanker, was Holland's assessment.

The Home Office pathologist had been called to the scene. This was often beneficial to a murder investigation as it gave the pathologist a good feel for the scene and location and body before its eventual removal to a mortuary for post mortem. He was standing a few feet away from Leon's body, mumbling his observations into a portable digital recorder.

Holland tried to get a grip of himself before speaking to the guy.

'What've we got?'

The pathologist stopped recording and blew out his cheeks. 'A particularly brutal, violent death.'

Holland raised his eyes contemptuously, as if to say, 'Tell me something I don't know.'

'Death was caused by suffocation – not drowning in the conventional sense as you might suspect from the way it looks. His lungs will not be saturated with water, although there will be water in the lungs, of that I'm certain. What in essence has happened is suffocation similar to someone holding a pillow over your face. In this case, though, the airways have been blocked by water rather than a pillow, if you see what I mean? That is how the death has been caused. The skull has filled with water and eventually the eyes have burst out of their sockets, rather like a pair of those joke glasses you can buy at funfairs. Eyes on springs, you know?'

'Yes, I know.'

'He did also try to struggle free – desperately – as you can see from the terrible cuts in his feet and ankles caused by the barbed wire, but he was so expertly bound that he had little room to move or manoeuvre and dislodge the tube, which I think I will find a few inches down his throat. A terrible death.'

Holland exhaled a long sigh and said, 'Bollocks.'

His mobile phone rang. It was an analyst from the Intelligence Unit confirming that PC Tony Griffin had also accessed the file relating to Leon Romes a few days earlier.

And now Leon was dead.

Holland hung up, thinking, 'Got you now, you bastard.' He looked at the dead piece of meat that was the carcass of Leon Romes, and said, 'All I need do now is catch you.'

++++

SEVENTEEN

'Come on man, where the fuck are ya?' Rob had his mobile phone crushed to his ear, calling Leon's number which continually went onto voice mail. Rob shook the phone with frustration as he stalked along and down the slope into an underpass which was only dimly lit and probably a frightening place for most people. For Rob, it was his hunting ground, the typical sort of location where he did his street business and it held no fear for him. He was a denizen of this place, it was like a watering hole to him and he was the lion in the long grass. He had robbed in it, kicked people half to death in it and dealt drugs in it. He knew every inch of it, knew which of the lights didn't work, knew where the shadows were and how to hide in them

That said, Leon's disappearance was having a bad effect on him.

Since their pact to split up and lie low, he hadn't heard from him. Yeah, they'd decided to keep apart, but also to stay in touch. Leon hadn't, which was a worry. He was probably the most vulnerable member of the crew, tough on the streets but a soft cunt underneath.

Rob had been to his brother's flat to get his head down, and that had been a good thing to do because Rob's brother was totally disassociated from the life Rob led. He worked hard in a 'normal' job, had a kid and a pretty girlfriend and lived in a domestic bliss that Rob despised. Not for him nappies and kid vomit.

But his brother always provided a good bolthole and always received him with love and generosity, although the girlfriend was wary of him. Rob frightened her and didn't mind if he did. She would have shit herself if Rob had said 'Boo!' to her.

He'd had a good night on the blanket at his brother's and now he was back on home ground.

He'd been to check out Leon's mother's house and had been given short shrift by her hard boyfriend, but Rob did learn that Leon had spent some time there the day before and had not been seen since leaving early yesterday evening, after having had a kip. Neither Leon's mum or boyfriend cared a shit.

And then there was a complete lack of response from Leon's phone.

Worrying.

Rob, in spite of his hard exterior, did have a soft spot for Leon – as he had for Josh, Warren's brother – so he felt it was his responsibility to track him down and make sure he was okay. Not least because Rob was also thinking of the future, and that it would be stupid not to move into the position vacated by Warren. It was time for Rob to step up to the mark. But he needed Leon behind him, so where was the twat?

Stepping into the underpass, Rob entered a world of silence. The sound of the traffic from the dual carriageway above was sliced off and there was nothing but the echo of his own footsteps because no one else was down there.

Except, as he reached mid-point, Rob spun around, thinking he had heard something behind him.

Nothing.

'Shit,' Rob breathed. He was beginning to scare himself shitless. Tales of the Ripper.

He paused and peered carefully into the shadows that were once his, saw nothing, turned and headed off, and walked straight into Jimmy Vickers who had somehow – somehow – appeared from nowhere.

'Fuc...'

Rob's instinct, forged by a life on the street, made him swing instantly at the figure in front of him, but Jimmy ducked under its arc and launched a haymaker into Rob's face, hard and accurate, sending him staggering backward, stunned and uncoordinated. Jimmy stepped with him, grabbed his throat and like dancing some ghoulish tango, he ran him back up against the underpass wall, which was covered with bad graffiti. His head cracked sickeningly and the combination of the two blows, the punch from the front, the bang from the back, seemed to collide with a loud explosion somewhere in the centre of Rob's brain.

Then Jimmy had the Sig in his hand, had stuffed it hard into Rob's cheek, cutting the soft inner flesh against his teeth. Rob tasted salty blood.

Jimmy's other hand cupped Rob's face, distorting his features.

'Open your mouth, open your mouth.'

Jimmy squeezed his face, forcing Rob to open his mouth and then he punched the barrel of the pistol inside Rob's mouth, breaking teeth.

***

'Now, fucker, you understand exactly what you have to do, don't you?'

Jimmy was speaking into Rob's ear, the muzzle of the Sig now skewered into Rob's neck just behind his right ear. Rob's left arm was twisted so far up his back, between his shoulder blades he could have almost scratched his head. All Jimmy had to do was ease it another few centimetres and the shoulder would simply pop out of its socket. As it was, it was screamingly painful anyway and Rob felt like his ligaments were being torn from their moorings.

Rob nodded. Sweat poured from his skull.

His face was now a beaten mess, because Jimmy couldn't resist, but knew just how far to take it. Far enough to achieve complete control.

Only minutes later, he had manoeuvred Rob all the way from the underpass, up the tower block and onto the corridor on which was the door to Caleb's flat.

Jimmy moved Rob's arm just a little further up his back.

'Yeah man, I know,' Rob winced.

Jimmy began to move Rob forward, keeping him under total control, marching him along the corridor, up to Caleb's door. Jimmy stepped back slightly, bent a little out of sight by using Rob as a screen, then forced the gun harder into the back of Rob's head at the point where his skull balanced on his spine.

'Knock.'

Rob did.

Eventually, a voice responded from the other side, muffled. Not Caleb.

'Fuck is it?'

'Rob.'

There was a groan of annoyance, then a long pause. Jimmy held Rob in place. Then the voice came back, 'Caleb says you've got five seconds before he comes out and shoots...'

Jimmy prodded the muzzle hard, prompting Rob.

'Come on, man ... open up, just wanna talk...'

***

Caleb's security man was the tattooed beast of a man who had, not very long ago, although it seemed forever, escorted Rob, Leon and Danny into the flat after they had lost Josh in Cash4Gold to the old man's baseball bat blow to the head that had killed him.

He was the one who had just conveyed Rob's presence at the door to Caleb, then returned the less than friendly message back.

Caleb, it seemed, was not interested in Rob, but Rob's little whine had annoyed the security man, so he made the very bad mistake of opening the door after glancing through the spyhole and just seeing Rob there with his face smashed in. Curiosity got the better of him and he unlocked the door and opened it – and the door, of course, was not secured by a chain, because this had been cut in half when Rob and Leon had had the effrontery to burst in and challenge Caleb. It hung useless, not having been replaced.

As the door opened an inch, Jimmy removed the gun from Rob's neck and opened fire.

Four rounds burst through the door and each round smacked into the security man's torso, making him do an ungraceful shimmy as they drove into him, two into his belly, two into his upper chest. Though they had lost much of their force, having passed through the door, there was enough killing power in them to tear his organs to shreds and kill him.

He sat down with a thump, then sagged sideways against the inner hallway wall, blood gushing from the mortal wounds.

As this was happening, Jimmy – still very much in control of Rob – twisted him to one side and flat-footed the door, which crashed open. Jimmy jerked Rob back in front of him and stormed into the hallway so quickly that the security man had just slumped dead.

At the far end of the hall, Caleb and another of his lieutenants were at the door of the counting room, side by side, both armed as a matter of course with handguns. Caleb's was a good gun, a Russian made pistol, very serviceable. His lieutenant's was a converted piece of crap, totally inaccurate from a distance, but deadly close up.

Both opened fire as Jimmy brought Rob back in front of him as a human shield.

Rob screamed desperately, 'Wait, wait.'

A bullet struck him in the shin. He roared in agony, suddenly becoming a non-compliant deadweight to Jimmy, who struggled to hold him upright. He hauled him to one side but had to drop him. He loosed off several shots at Caleb and the other man, having to step over the body of the dead security man as well as Rob.

Jimmy twirled into the first room on his right – a bedroom – then loosed off two more shots down the hall from the cover of the doorway. These took out Caleb's man with both rounds piercing his chest and heart, leaving Caleb still alive. Jimmy dodged back out of sight, calculating how many rounds he had discharged in that opening salvo. Ten. Five remained in the magazine. He had a spare mag in his waistband.

Rob, meanwhile, driven by self-preservation, half-scrambled and stumbled out of the flat and was gone, leaving a trail of blood behind him.

Jimmy cursed, then stepped out from the cover of the bedroom.

Caleb had disappeared, no sign of him down the hallway.

Jimmy waited. His breathing was calm and measured, his heart rate very much under control.

And waiting was his forte.

The waiting gap was the one the others always had to fill, either with words or actions.

People like Caleb, who might be the soldiers of the streets in their eyes, but in reality they knew little about real combat.

On cue, Caleb took a look, not expecting to see Jimmy.

And with the best will in the world, a drug dealer and Fagin type figure going up against someone as well trained and disciplined as James Vickers was really no match. The outcome was sealed.

Caleb reacted to the vision of Jimmy. Too slowly.

It was almost a formality for Jimmy to shoot him, the only problem for Jimmy being that he didn't want to kill Caleb yet. He had other plans for him. He shot him in the thigh and the upper right quadrant of his chest. Caleb fell back into the counting room.

The sound of the shots echoed away.

Jimmy did not move. His eyes took in the dead body of the security man; down the hall the feet of Caleb's other man poked out of the door, twitching macabrely and somewhere beyond, out of sight, Jimmy heard Caleb moaning.

Still Jimmy did not move.

Sixth sense: Something not quite right.

In a parallel thought he recalculated the number of rounds he had left: three.

Suddenly someone stepped into that waiting gap again. The difference between an amateur and a professional.

Kadie, Caleb's magnificent girlfriend swung into view. Completely naked, large pendulous breasts, shaved pubic area, tattoos.

The only thing she sported was the sawn-off, pump action shotgun, which she unleashed down the corridor – BOOM! There was the click-clack as she worked the pump action and another shell slid into the breach immediately – and BOOM! She racked the gun again and reloaded.

Jimmy moved the instant he saw her emerge, flinging himself into the bedroom, feeling the whoosh of the buckshot pass him and disrupt the air where he had been standing. He also took the opportunity to reload, letting the magazine slide out and then slapping in the full spare one. He literally saw the second shot from the shotgun fly past down the hall.

Now he knew she was waiting for his reappearance with her aim locked on his position, looking down the barrel, ready to blow off his head.

'Stick your head out you fucker, I dare you,' she even challenged him.

Not one to refuse such a dare, Jimmy popped his head out and drew it back in straight away. It was enough to make her jerk the trigger back and fire. She missed Jimmy, but the blast of the cartridge tore out a great chunk of the door frame where Jimmy's head had been.

In that instant, she knew she had made a fatal error, should not have fired – because now she had to reload.

She did it as quickly as possible, but Jimmy was faster. As she racked the weapon, Jimmy stepped out into the hallway and while still moving, he double tapped two rounds into Kadie's head, effectively removing the upper back quarter of her shaved skull, killing her instantly, splattering the wall behind the counting table with her blood and mashed up brains.

Jimmy lowered his weapon. 'You didn't tell me about her,' Jimmy said, chastising Rob, who he would catch up with later.

He kicked shut the flat door.

***

Jimmy stepped into the counting room, stood over Caleb and kicked his gun away. Caleb watched him in silence now, with baleful eyes, wincing when pain corkscrewed through his body from his wounds, wondering what was next.

Jimmy hauled Caleb across the room, dragging his legs over Kadie's stomach, making her wobble obscenely. Her breasts, magnificent in life, were deflated and ugly in death. Jimmy pulled Caleb over to the counting table and slung him on a chair and forced his head down onto the table top, holding him in place. Caleb tried to struggle, but his wounds had made him weak and Jimmy also warned, 'Don't.'

The blood from Caleb's chest spread quickly across the table top, so that very soon the side of his head was resting in it. He tried to move again, but Jimmy forced the muzzle of the Sig into his head and said, 'Don't,' once more.

***

Caleb's head lay sideways in his own blood on the table top, but now it was duct-taped to the table itself and his wrists were taped to his ankles.

Jimmy worked his way through the kitchen cupboards, searching for Caleb's chemicals and finding what he needed, bleach and ammonia. He came back into the counting room and placed a bucket on the floor beside Caleb's feet, ensuring that Caleb could see what was happening, including the fact that Jimmy was now wearing protective gloves and goggles and a dust mask with a breathing valve over his nose and mouth.

Jimmy scraped all of Caleb's packages of coke and tabs into the bucket, then began to mix the bleach and ammonia in it. The contents started to fizz as the chemicals mixed together and formed hydrochloric acid. Noxious fumes started to rise.

'Listen man,' Caleb said, finding it almost impossible to make his words because of the tape holding his head to the table and that he was speaking through his own blood. 'I don't know what the fuck your problem is, mate, or who's paying you, but I'll treble it, Bruv. Treble it,' he reiterated. 'See that safe there, take the lot, man.

Jimmy glanced over at the safe in the corner of the room, sitting on the floor but riveted to the wall. He walked to it. 'What's the code?' His voice was muffled by the mask.

'Na, na, let me up first mate.' Caleb coughed as the fumes from the bucket hit the back of his throat. Even so, he had already decided that he would take Jimmy when he was set free, gunshot wounds or not. He would find the strength from somewhere to rip this fucker's head off.

Jimmy shrugged, walked back to Caleb, who coughed again.

'Alright,' he relented. 'You gotta promise me you'll let me go, yeah?'

Jimmy nodded.

'Twenty-one, six, forty-four.'

Jimmy tapped in the number and the safe door swung open.

It was stacked to bursting with wads and wads of notes, crushed in. Jimmy took them and made his way back to the table. He held them so that Caleb could see and very deliberately dropped them into the bucket.

Caleb groaned, defeated. No escape, no compromise. 'No, no, no, fuck man, what do ya want?'

'Someone else who doesn't know,' Jimmy said, then rammed a wad of notes into Caleb's mouth, silencing him.

Caleb spat them out, struggled, but in so doing he started to breathe more heavily, inhaling more and more of the toxic chloramine fumes from the bucket. They went down the back of his throat like acid, burning, scorching his trachea and lungs and he started to convulse, choking to death.

Jimmy waited patiently until Caleb was still, then tipped the hydrochloric acid slowly onto Caleb's head. It started to fizzle, smoke rising from his skin as the acid burned. Then Jimmy tipped on some more and Caleb's head began to disintegrate and liquefy until it was nothing more than a mush, with the consistency of a rotted potato.

Once the bucket was empty, Jimmy left the flat. No remorse.

++++

Jimmy (Danny Dyer) searches the crack den for drug dealer
Caleb

Caleb's beautiful girlfriend Kadie (Tiffanni Thompson) has
murder on her mind

EIGHTEEN

Julia Greaves sat opposite her computer screen in her office, divided from the mayhem that was the offices of the London Today newspaper by glass partition walls. She was typing in a very desultory way, cowed a little by the overbearing presence of her editor, Elliot Grant hovering behind her, holding a sheet of paper in his hand.

Grant sighed despondently as he read out, referring in passing to the paper. 'The UK could face austerity until 2018 – duh. Jules, this is borderline cat stuck up a tree, babe.' His new sigh was one of desperation.

Julia shrugged her shoulders, on the defensive. 'Elliot, Marcus is on the NHS cover-up, Natalie's on the tube strike and other than that, London's quiet.'

'What about these murders? You were coming in your panties the other day.'

'Hit a brick wall on it, nothing on-going,' she hated to admit.

'Thought you had a new lead?'

'I did. Just waiting to get a bit more substance on it.'

'Well don't wait. Abi is already sniffing to snatch it from you. Whatever you're sitting on, let's be having it – publish and be damned.'

When Grant left, she sat back and mulled it over for a few minutes, marshalling her thoughts. Then she went for old glory, typing furiously, pen in mouth, adjusting and scribbling notes on her pad at the same time. Doing exactly what a hack does.

***

Spencer Holland picked up the first edition of London Today from his local newsagent before piling back into his car and heading back to the nick.

The traffic was mind-bogglingly slow and at the third set of lights he reached which were on red – and certain that some bastard up in the traffic control centre was having a laugh at his expense – he picked up the paper and glanced with disinterest at the headline.

"JUSTICE OR TERRORISM? VIGILANTE STRIKES AGAIN!"

The words were big, bold, and as effective as a 'V' sign jerked up into Holland's face.

He fired the paper across the car in a burst of rage.

'Bitch.'

He tried desperately to compose himself, but failed miserably. He vented his fury on the steering wheel, pounding the crap out of it whilst screaming, 'Bitch! Bitch! Bitch! Bitch!'

His tirade could be heard from the footpath and several pedestrians gawped at him, then walked swiftly on.

Just another nut job out of control in London.

***

Not too far away in another area of London, Big Ben struck four – in time with each punch Holland delivered to his steering wheel.

But in that area, the capital was being its usual stereotypical self without any hint of irony or self-awareness. It just was London, in some respects a relic of a bygone age. Black cabs, open-topped red tour buses passing the Cenotaph, the fast-sinking sun striking the intricately built walls of Westminster Abbey and Big Ben pushing towards the darkening sky. The roads were crammed with traffic, the pavements with scurrying people, all walking far too quickly, each on their own solitary journey, living their blocked lives. All that was missing was the bowler hat brigade and pinstriped suits on city types, walking across Westminster Bridge.

This stereotype could be followed into the offices of power somewhere deep in Whitehall, where some of the corridors still had polished teak panels and sturdy doors with shining brass handles, Almost frozen in a time that once existed, but was now just preserved for posterity.

At the end of a long, wide corridor sat Chief Superintendent Dennis Walsh alongside his ultimate boss, Commissioner Shields, a thickset, stern man with intelligent eyes and an air of confidence about him.

Both were in full uniform, looked smart.

They sat in silence.

They had been summoned.

A door opened silently on well-oiled hinges at the far end of the corridor and a man in a sombre suit approached the two officers. His name was Carter. He was in his late fifties, had a military bearing, his steel grey hair cut short, matching the colour of his eyes.

His approach seemed to last forever, like some sort of optical illusion.

Finally, he reached the two officers and extended his hand to Shields, recognisable instantly by the 'bird shit' on his uniform, a crown above a Bath star (or pip) above crossed tipstaves on his epaulettes, the man in absolute charge of the Metropolitan Police ... sort of. Carter said, 'Commissioner Shields, I presume.'

They shook hands and Shields said yes.

Carter then shook hands with Walsh in a more offhand manner. His insignia was a single crown above a Bath star and he was lower in rank.

'I'm Chief Superintendent Walsh,' Walsh said quickly and Carter nodded.

'Follow me, gentlemen.'

Carter turned and headed back down the corridor, more quickly than his previous journey in the opposite direction.

'I didn't get your name,' Shields said.

'Carter.'

'Would that be Mister Carter?'

'It would be Chief of Staff Carter,' he said briskly, and Shields then knew they were here to be put firmly in their place. He had been to such encounters before. He had always fought his corner and sometimes he'd won and sometimes he'd backed off gracefully. It was the nature of the game, which was inevitably intertwined with politics and the needs of other agencies. You didn't get to be the highest ranking cop in the country without knowing when to retreat, attack or compromise.

They arrived at the door Carter had emerged from, which opened to reveal a very spacious and plush office with a single, oval shaped, oak table at its centre. Bulletproof windows overlooked Whitehall below.

Three stern looking men sat at the table, all much the same age, fifties.

Shields hesitated and Walsh glanced at him, both wondering, 'What the fuck?'

Carter circumnavigated the table and gestured for the two officers to take seats opposite the three men, with a 'Please.'

They sat, both feeling this was going to like a very tough promotion board.

The man in the middle of the trio was clearly the leader. He was very finely suited, and even before he opened his mouth, Shields and Walsh knew that he owned this space. They didn't know his name, nor did he offer it up. They didn't know which government department he represented.

His name was actually Rooker.

His initial opening was conciliatory and without sarcasm. 'Thank you for coming at such short notice, gentlemen. You will have to forgive our somewhat hasty pace on this matter, but we must get straight to the point without preamble.'

Laid in front of him was a brown military file, stapled to the outside cover of which was a passport-sized photograph of Jimmy Vickers.

Rooker pushed the file across the wide table, Walsh rotated it so he and Shields could see it.

'Jimmy Vickers – he's a suspect in a series of murders,' Walsh said.

Rooker and the man to his right shared a glance. Then Rooker said to the police officers, 'At no point can this man be taken into police custody. Is that understood?'

Shields had had enough. His patience was gone already. He looked at the file and Jimmy's photograph, then up at Rooker. 'Perhaps we can dispense with the cloak and dagger stuff here and start over,' he said firmly. 'I'm Commissioner Shields from the Metropolitan Police, the head of the Met Police, actually – and you are?'

'The man who makes sure you and the rest of this exquisite country are safe every second of every day,' Rooker said frostily, avoiding the answer.

Carter stepped in, hoping to clear the air of the obvious tension. 'We feel somewhat embarrassed that this individual has slipped our grasp, but I assure you, Commissioner, he belongs to us. Your man heading up this investigation will report his progress on the hour and you will report to us. Is that clear?'

Walsh nodded, but Shields still wasn't happy. He had been dragged away from a huge backlog of work to appear in this office and he was not going to be dictated about operational issues by people he didn't even know what jobs they did, or what authority they operated under. He knew it would no doubt override anything he had, but he still wasn't happy. He wanted to know. This had to be a two way street, or no deal. He could be just as obstinate as anyone.

'Just throw us a bone here, guys,' he said. 'Not much to ask, is it?'

The three men on the panel glanced at each other and came to a silent agreement.

Opposite them, Walsh had opened Jimmy's file.

Rooker pursed his lips and said, 'He works for a unit within the confines of our military infrastructure that benefits from a certain character profile, shall we say?'

'SAS?' Shields asked.

Carter shot a look at Rooker: beware.

'He is a problem that you don't want on your streets, a problem that only we can deal with – and we need him back where he belongs.'

***

Everyone else was asked to leave, and when they'd gone Rooker stood by the net curtains looking down on Whitehall. Shields stood alongside him, troubled.

'I need to know who this Jimmy Vickers is.'

Rooker sighed, knowing that he had to tell because it was imperative the Met were on side with this. He took a moment to compose his words.

'Not a word of this leaves the room,' he warned. Shields nodded.

Rooker announced, '7/7 could have been averted. Went down to the wire. We were trying to get information out of this greasy Abdullah up until an hour before the attacks. We pressed him and we pressed hard. But could we get him to talk?' Rooker shook his head, answering his own rhetorical question. Distantly he said, 'We lost London that day … our capital won't fall again, not like that. After 7/7 a programme was commissioned that would grant the means to extract information from terror suspects using whatever means possible, and anywhere in the world. Enhanced Information Extraction Techniques, EIET. You may have heard whispers of it – or not. It would give certain soldiers privileges to get the information we need to protect this country. Fast, efficient and brutal, and there is only one military unit you give that sort of power to.'

'SAS,' Shields guessed again.

Rooker neither confirmed nor denied that. Instead, he said, 'Vickers's character profile appeared perfect for the role … and it was … but with recent events that included the death of his parents, it's safe to say he's gone…' Rooker searched for the appropriate word.

'Mad?' Shields chose for him.

'Rogue,' Rooker corrected him. 'Jimmy Vickers is not mad. Far from it.'

'If this law, or programme was passed, and I presume in secret at the highest levels, then why was Vickers arrested by your authorities in the first place?' Shields queried.

'Went too far. A dead prisoner is a dead prisoner, especially in a hospital. Goes without saying that is frowned upon … but he holds some vital intelligence in his head that we need – urgently.'

'But it's okay to chop off fingers and stick needles in testicles?'

'That,' Rooker said sadly, 'is war, my friend.'

***

Holland's phone rang over the speakers in his car. Before answering, he checked the caller ID: Chief Superintendent Walsh. Still fuming, Holland chilled and attempted cheerfulness. 'Sir, how the hell are you?'

'Spencer – have you seen the freakin' newspaper?' Walsh blasted.

Immediately on guard, Holland lied smoothly, 'What newspaper is that?'

'Do not fuck with me … we've got a real big problem. No questions, but from now on I want you to report to me on the hour regarding this Jimmy Vickers thing.'

'Yes sir,' Holland frowned.

'You corner him, you call it in. You don't get brave. You wrap this up, and you wrap it up now, you hear me?'

Fuck me, stressed or what? Holland thought. 'Yes, sir, but I think we should…'

'On the hour,' Walsh snapped and hung up, no explanation given.

Before Holland even had the chance to curse, the phone rang again. 'What?'

***

How he escaped he would never know, but Rob's survival instinct kicked in the instant he took the bullet in the leg and then Vickers found himself unable to keep him held upright. Rob dropped like a brick as the bullets flew and the shootout raged between the two factions.

Unable to believe the barrage of rounds missed him, Rob half-crawled, half-dragged himself out of the flat and down the corridor, where he scuttled on his hands and knees, leaving a trail of blood behind him from the wound in the lower leg which in those initial moments just felt numb.

He reached the door that was the emergency exit, reached up for the release bar and fell through into a narrow landing at the top of the stairs, then pitched headlong down the concrete steps, coming to an untidy heap at the first turn of the steps. Dazed, hurt, he fell down the next set of steps, and did not stop going. To do so, he knew, would have been fatal.

He stood up, tried his weight on his leg, at which point the numbness turned to agony. The leg gave way under him and he fell down the next set of steps with a scream of pain and hit the next landing so hard the impact drove all his breath out of him.

Gasping and now in indescribable pain – which radiated up from the bullet wound – Rob pushed himself on.

This time, he sat on the top step of the next set and thudded down on his arse, like he was tobogganing, each drop onto his bony bottom jarring his body and he was forced to clamp a hand over his mouth to muffle his own cries.

Eventually he made it to the bottom of the stairwell, having left an easy to follow trail of blood.

Then he limped out into the night, hobbling and holding himself upright against walls and railings, forcing himself to keep moving instead of acquiescing to the overpowering urge just to curl up and give in, die. He knew that distance and time were his allies in this retreat and the more he had of both, the more chance he had of living. And, maybe, revenge.

Finally, he had to stop. Weakness pervaded his system. The adrenaline rush that had helped him so far had gone. He was exhausted and in agonising pain.

He staggered into an alley and lifted the lid of an industrial size wheelie bin. He clambered over the edge and dropped into the foetid bed of rotting food, bin bags and general waste inside. He didn't care. He had to rest. There was nothing left in him and he drifted into a hazy state, somewhere on the cusp of consciousness and oblivion.

Next thing he knew he was experiencing a strange, rising sensation, a sway of movement; the sound of diesel motors, a sudden stop, tilt, jerk and then he was falling into a morass of overpowering stench. Strangely it felt good and Rob wondered if this was what death was like. Had he died? If he had, it wasn't so bad. It was soft and squishy. Maybe the disgusting odour meant he had gone to hell.

It was the harsh Cockney voice that made him realise he was still very much in the land of the living, when the bin man shouted, 'Stop the motor, mate, stop the motor. We got a fuckin' body in this one.'

***

Holland abandoned his car in the yellow hatch markings reserved for ambulances only outside the A&E department. A paramedic sliding a trolley back inside an ambulance turned to remonstrate.

'Oi – ambulances only.'

'I'm a cop and the car stays here.' Holland flashed his warrant card and strode past the open-mouthed paramedic and called back over his shoulder, 'And if anyone touches it, I'll snap their fuckin' heads off.'

And then he was gone. He was annoyed briefly as the sliding doors hesitated for a moment too long for him before opening and allowing him through into the casualty department.

The unit, as ever, was heaving. A scrolling LED message board informed patients of a '3 Hour Wait' followed by a smiley face.

Holland pushed through to the reception desk, still flashing his ID.

He had to wait an irritating two minutes before the doctor came to see him and then led him through the A&E ward which was divided up into a series of curtained cubicles.

As he walked, the doctor explained, 'Gunshot wound to lower right leg but not serious. The bullet has basically nicked the muscle, sort of gouged a line through it, but you think he'd been shot in the chest from the way he's complaining about it. Here…'

The doctor yanked back a curtain.

A very sorry looking Rob looked up through puppy eyes at Holland. His leg was wrapped in a bandage. A nurse stood next to him, easing a drip into the vein in the back of his right hand.

'Leave us,' Holland ordered the medical staff. The nurse glanced at the doctor, who nodded. The nurse taped the needle in place, adjusted the flow on the drip and left, scowling at Holland, who ignored her, entered the cubicle and closed the curtain.

The two men eyed each other.

'We need to talk,' Holland said.

'About what?' Rob snarled sourly.

'You and me,' Holland smiled, 'have the same goal.'

++++

Chief Superintendent Walsh (Sam Kane) briefs Spencer Holland (Alistair Petrie) on the situation with Jimmy Vickers and the SAS

Sinister Whitehall mandarin Rooker (Bruce Payne) flanked by Chief of Staff Carter (Hugo Myatt)

NINETEEN

He had been here before, but the last time he had entered through the front door after having driven a screwdriver into the eye of the bastard who had killed Josh. Now he was returning, coming at the house from the rear. He stood in the shadow by the back fence, looking, checking, taking his time. This had to be right.

In his right hand, a jemmy dangled by his thigh. He crouched, then stalked across the lawn to the back door. Limping, but feeling no great pain, the morphine and other pain killers doing a great job, together with the four lines of coke he'd just snorted. Then he was at the patio door which he jemmied open with one, expert crack, then he was in the house.

He stood still and waited.

The smell of the fire that had gutted the garage still pervaded the house. The place where the couple had died.

Rob moved slowly around the house from one room to the next, initially doing nothing, just looking, taking it all in.

He began to look properly, a pen light torch held in his mouth.

The family photographs on the walls. Happy times. Old wedding photographs. Rob recognised the younger version of the dead couple, one with a Harley Davidson motorbike in it, the bride posing on it, her wedding dress pulled up her shapely leg, revealing the intricate garter.

Rob smirked, recalling how Warren had fucked her arse till she bled.

Happy times.

Then other photographs. One in which the wife was cradling a new born baby. One with a young lad in it wearing boxing gloves that were ludicrously big, standing next to a punch bag and holding a trophy between the gloves. Rob recognised the face of the kid. Their son. A face that reappeared in more happy family photographs, including one that was probably quite recent. The old couple with the young man between them, maybe taken a year ago, with the son planting a kiss on the woman's cheek. There was also a photo of the son on his wedding day, with a bride who looked stunningly beautiful.

Rob inspected this photograph for a long time.

'Jimmy fuckin' Vickers,' he hissed through his teeth clenched on the torch.

Next, Rob raided cabinets, chests of drawers and cupboards.

He pulled out a stack of envelopes from a drawer addressed to James Vickers, care of this address. Rob tore them open, reading carefully. One was an official A4 sized envelope with County Court divorce papers in them, unsigned. He moved into the hallway and found an address book next to the telephone. He leafed through it and saw a written entry next to 'Jimmy & Morgan'. Pure gold.

Rob had one more thing to do before leaving. He went into the garage and saw the charred punch bag still hanging in place from the garage ceiling.

Rob pissed on it.

***

Rob sank low into the car seat as the woman walked past him. She did not clock him but walked up the driveway into her house. His pistol was resting between his thighs. Out of habit, he checked that it was loaded.

***

Rob needed a drink desperately. The pain killers, morphine and coke had dehydrated him and he needed water. He parked up on an area of land near to his dive of a flat and limped to the corner shop to buy some, swigging it greedily as he climbed back in the car. He had things he needed to do. He finished the drink, scrunched up the bottle and tossed it out of the window.

He had not noticed the figure sitting silently behind him in the back seat.

Rob inserted his key into the ignition, started the engine and adjusted the rear view mirror – and almost leapt out of his skin.

'We meet again.'

Jimmy stuffed the barrel of his Sig into Rob's exposed neck. Rob's hands came up automatically. 'Alright, alright … what d'ya want, mate?'

'I wanna go for a drive this time.'

'Where?'

'I'll tell you where. Just drive.'

Rob turned to face the front and adjusted his clothing, slyly switching on the GPS beacon in his jacket pocket. It started to transmit his position. Not how he had wanted it to pan out, but so be it.

***

Holland pushed his arms into his Kevlar vest and fastened it over his suit. He was strutting along a ground floor corridor in the police station and behind him was the SFO team, all fully kitted out, overalls, gloves, vests, boots, Kevlar skull caps, goggles, radios and of course their weapons. The Glock 17s, MP5 submachine guns – some with shotguns, all with Tasers and batons. A heavy load of kit carried by a very fit bunch of men and women.

Holland stormed ahead in front of them to the police car park. They peeled off into various vehicles which, on Holland's command – as he was in the lead vehicle – screeched out onto the road.

Holland's face was set hard with triumph. Tonight, he was going to secure his reputation and his future.

And Jimmy Vickers was his meal ticket.

***

Rob turned onto an unmade gravel area by the Thames, near Limehouse. He pulled to a halt on the empty piece of land, boarded on three sides by disused warehouses in a location ripe for development but just lacking the money to do so.

A location just right for an execution.

Following Jimmy's orders, Rob killed the engine.

Jimmy moved quickly, silently, and moments later Rob was on his knees, hands tied behind his back, the plastic cable ties digging into his wrists.

Jimmy stood arrogantly in front of him, then crouched low, so they were at eye level.

In his right hand he had a hypodermic needle which he pierced into a tiny phial of clear liquid, drew back the plunger and filled the needle with the substance in front of Rob's eyes.

'What's that?'

'This,' – Jimmy held up the bottle and needle – 'is sarin. At its most dangerous in aerosol form, sprayed into the atmosphere as a gas, it can kill hundreds. You vomit, you have spasms, your insides feel like they're on fire. In liquid form, like this, injected into the vein, it slows the process down. You're going to be begging me to put a bullet into you...any last words?'

'Fuck you! I pissed on your parents.' Rob spat into Jimmy's face.

Jimmy wiped his face and carefully placed down the needle and phial. Rob watched this measured reaction with trepidation.

Jimmy rounded a punch into the side of Rob's face, sending him over onto the ground. Jimmy laid into him, unrelenting and cold. Kicking him hard, feeling his ribs crack. Then he dragged him upright and balanced him, Rob spluttering and coughing blood, which also poured from a cut in his scalp line.

Rob still taunted him. 'Feel better now? Ey? You dickhead. You feel better now?'

Jimmy squatted back down. 'Did you?'

Through cut and swollen lips, Rob smiled dangerously. 'I will, mate.' Jimmy blinked, not understanding him.

'Eh?'

Rob laughed coarsely. 'I will – when I see your face in a minute.' He spat a gob of blood, which dribbled obscenely down his chin. 'I'm gonna feel so much better.'

'Fuck you talkin' about?' Jimmy sneered, experiencing a sensation of dread. Something was very wrong here.

'You got in the back of my car didn't ya? Thinkin' you was holdin' all the cards, you mug. But you ain't got fuck all ... Jimmy fucking Vickers. How long have we been driving for, ten, twenty minutes?' Rob pulled back his lips, snarling with his blood-stained teeth. 'Didn't even know, did ya? Didn't even know what was in the boot of the car.' He cackled madly.

Jimmy stood up slowly and made his way to the back of the car, his chest tightening.

Reluctantly, he pushed the button and the boot lid rocked open.

'No,' he whispered.

Morgan's naked body lay there, folded into the boot, wrapped in clear plastic sheeting, her wide open dead eyes looking imploringly at Jimmy.

Rob was laughing hysterically now. 'Fucking feisty one, she was mate,' he called out callously. 'Put up a great fight, but I still raped the shit out of her before I strangled her. Thought her fuckin' eyeballs were gonna pop out. Her tongue did, went purple.'

Jimmy could not tear his eyes away from her. And then he saw it: the wedding ring on her finger which sent him to his knees, tears streaming. 'No, no.' His rage built. 'No.'

Rob screamed with manic laughter.

Jimmy went silent, then stood up and walked slowly to Rob, standing before him, channelling his emotions.

He hit Rob hard in the face, picked him up, hit him again. Picked him up again, set him straight, although by now Rob's head was lolling and uncontrolled.

That was enough.

Jimmy took a step back, drew the Sig from his waistband and aimed at Rob's chest.

He fired three times. Rob's front exploded with the impact of each shot and he slumped over onto the gravel, gasping for his final breaths as the blood and oxygen formed bubbles at the wounds and blood gushed up his throat and out of his mouth.

Jimmy stood over him, his form menacing, watching Rob die, and a dreadful cocktail of feelings churning through him like the vortex of a storm.

***

The cops moved in fast and efficiently, racing around the corner from behind one of the deserted factory units, fanning out in a coordinated, pre-planned and well-rehearsed movement, giving Jimmy Vickers nowhere to run.

The SFO leader screamed, 'Armed Police! Put the weapon down. Put the weapon down.'

Jimmy looked around slowly, the Sig hanging loosely at his side, his chest heaving. He did not drop it.

A line of armed cops edged towards him, inexorably boxing him in.

Jimmy glanced at his gun.

From behind the police line, DCI Spencer Holland squeezed through, smug, very proud of himself, and confronted Jimmy.

Another car hurtled onto the gravel, flicking up dust and grime as it swerved and skidded to a stop. Half of the firearms team snapped around, brought their weapons to bear on the driver as he jumped out.

It was Griff, having been kept abreast of developments and hoping to somehow save Jimmy from being shot dead. As he jumped out, he saw Morgan's body in the boot of Rob's car, saw Rob dead on the ground. And with horror, worked it all out.

'Wait,' Griff shouted. 'Wait.'

Holland glanced Griff's way, then walked confidently towards Jimmy – who stood there unmoving, other than for the rise and fall of his chest and the pain etched on his face.

Holland was loving this. 'I'm gonna give you to the count of three, Vickers … one…'

Griff ran at Holland and grabbed his jacket. The firearms team followed this development.

'Who the fuck do you think you are?' Griff demanded.

Holland brushed him away like he was shit. 'Don't you fucking touch me.'

Griff was relentless and emotional, almost crying. 'You had him in the hospital and you let him go, even though you knew what he'd done,' he screamed into Holland's face. 'You let him go and he killed his wife.'

The SFO leader reacted, turning his attention from Jimmy to the hostility between Holland and Griff.

Jimmy stood silent, taking it in.

'Go on,' Griff urged Holland, pointing accusingly towards Rob's car. 'Tell him you're the reason why his wife is dead in the boot of that car. Tell him.'

Cornered, Holland came out on the offensive. 'Yeah, I let him go. I let him go because I knew he would lead me to this fuckin' psychopath.' He jabbed his finger at Jimmy.

His words had an effect on the firearms team. A number of the weapons aimed and ready to fire and bring down Jimmy were lowered hesitantly and the team leader yanked off his protective helmet and goggles. It was Joe Windsor.

Holland noticed the reaction, felt the change in the atmosphere. Trying not to lose this, and justify himself, he blabbered, 'Yeah, I let him go. I didn't know he'd go and do that, did I? But y'know,' he shrugged uncaringly as though it was nothing, 'shit happens and it's what you gotta do to get the job done. Collateral damage.'

'Stand down,' Joe Windsor cut in, giving the order to his team. He'd heard enough and after having agonised about keeping Griff in the loop, he knew it had been the right thing to do.

'What the fuck do you think you're doing?' Holland shouted, getting more fraught as this whole scenario started to slip from his dirty grasp.

Joe held his radio pad to his neck and as he transmitted the next message to firearms control, he kept his eyes on Holland, unable to keep the disgust out of them. 'Alpha One to control … suspect has fled the scene on foot, repeat, suspect has fled the scene on foot.'

'Roger that, Alpha One,' control room replied.

Holland was astounded, gibbering with incandescent rage. 'What? Are you fucking insane? You're gonna let him walk?'

Suddenly Jimmy started walking towards the police line, which parted almost biblically to allow him to pass through. Aghast and shaking with fury, Holland stood by to watch him pass.

Jimmy did not look either way, just walked towards the road.

'I see,' Holland said. 'No one's gonna arrest him? Fuckin' fine! You want something done around here, you do it your fucking self.'

He snapped out his extendable baton with a swish and a crack, flicking it out to its full length and went after Jimmy.

No one stopped him. This was all now his play. His shit storm.

But Jimmy knew he was there. He stopped without warning, spun and brought up the Sig and aimed it into Holland's face.

Holland froze, his whole body icing through. This was what terror felt like.

Jimmy fully intended to pull the trigger and blow out Holland's brains, but at that moment, in the periphery of his vision, he saw Rob dead on the ground, the open boot of the car with Morgan's body in it, and caught Griff's pleading eyes.

He lowered his aim.

Holland exhaled with relief and the supercilious look came back onto his face.

Jimmy switched the gun into his left hand and with his right he powered his fist into Holland's weak jaw. It connected beautifully, Holland's neck snapped back, four teeth hit the back of his throat and he dropped to his knees in front of Jimmy.

Next thing he knew, he was on the ground, unable to move, though his eyes were open and he was watching the figure of Jimmy Vickers walking towards the blackness of night.

++++

Armed response unit leader Joe Windsor (Ricci Hartnett)
realises that Jimmy has been set up by Holland

Colonel Leach (Vincent Regan) discusses Jimmy's fate with
sinister Whitehall mandarin Mr Rooker (Bruce Payne)

EPILOGUE

'Well?'

Rooker asked the question standing in the exact same spot he had been in while giving the secret briefing to Commissioner Shields of the Met Police. Only now, Whitehall was deserted and a new day was just about to kick in. That said, it would be a long time before the sun rose

The man he had directed the question at came to stand by him.

'Well?' Rooker asked again.

'Found him,' Colonel Leach said.

'See to it he comes in this time.'

'I don't think he wants to.'

'Then I will have to put people on it that will help change his mind.'

'But they'll kill him,' Leach said.

'You've forced my hand, Colonel. He may think he can take on the police force, but if he thinks he can get the better of his own unit, then he has another think coming.'

Rooker pointedly looked sideways at Leach, eyebrows arched, his meaning unambiguous. Jimmy Vickers was a marked man.

***

And three thousand miles away to the west, that marked man, in a different time zone, a different city, was hoping to make some sense of his life. He needed to free up some assets, and this had necessitated a flight across the Atlantic Ocean, using a forged passport, visa and other documents compulsory for entry into the USA. A legacy of his time on certain operations for the regiment, when using his own name was not an option.

As he landed in New York, Jimmy Vickers knew he was just one step ahead of the game. His plan was to leapfrog even more, pushing on until he reached the end of the road. Wherever that might be.

Until he could access his assets during banking hours, he walked the streets of the city. He stood for a long time and gazed up at the neon lights of Times Square, blinking, overpowered by tiredness and sadness because his new beginning had been snatched cruelly away from him.

Morgan's words rang in his ears: 'Just get into a car and drive.'

That is what he was going to do … but for the time being, he walked the city and for no real reason turned into the stairway leading down to the deserted subway on the corner of 3rd Avenue and 96th Street.

Jimmy heard the screams before he saw anyone. Terrified screams of a woman, pleading, 'Get off of me, let me go, please, please.'

Jimmy kept going, walking down the white tiled steps onto an empty platform, his hands thrust deep into his pockets, shoulders hunched, and came across what was happening. Two punks pinning a tiny woman up against a pillar. One held her while the other went through her purse.

'Please stop, please let me go.'

'Shut the fuck up, bitch.' The man holding her clamped a big hand over the woman's mouth, looked up and saw Jimmy standing there.

'Oi,' Jimmy said.

The one with the purse turned, and their two wild, drug crazed faces stared at him. The guy flung the purse down and rose to his full height. He was a big man. 'Yo, what the fuck you want, asshole?'

'Yeah,' sneered the other, 'you gonna do something about this?' he said. He threw the woman to one side and she fell to her knees, sobbing and hurt.

'You got three seconds, muthafucka – turn round and walk the fuck back up them stairs man.' A switchblade suddenly appeared in this guy's hand. The both started to walk slowly and menacingly towards Jimmy, still there, hands deep in his pockets, resolute.

'One…'

Jimmy's chin was low into his neck, his face angled so he looked at them through his eyebrows.

'Two…'

An almost imperceptible smirk quivered on Jimmy's lips and turned into a slow, dangerous smile. The smile of the devil.

'THREE!'

++++

Coming soon from Caffeine Nights

The UK's most downloaded sports title of 2012
The Prequel to Top Dog

APPEARANCES CAN BE DECEPTIVE - as Paul Jarvis of the National Soccer Intelligence Unit is only too well aware. He knows that Billy Evans is no ordinary Cockney lad made good. He's also a thug, a villain and a cop killer. Jarvis just hasn't been able to prove it...

Yet.

So when Jarvis discovers that Evans is putting together a hooligan 'Super Crew' to follow the England national soccer team to Italy, he feels sure he can finally put Evans behind bars - if only someone can infiltrate the group and get him the proof he needs.

But nothing is ever that simple. The Crew believe Evans is just out for a full-on riot. Jarvis thinks he's trafficking drugs. But Billy Evans is always one step ahead. He has another plan. And it will be catastrophic for everyone concerned.

EXCEPT HIM

The Official Novelisation of the Movie

Sequel to the best-selling thriller, The Crew.

Soon to be a major motion picture starring Leo Gregory

GANG LEADER Billy Evans has ruled his turf in London for more years than he can care to remember. So long in fact, that even he realizes that things have become a little too easy.

So when an old adversary reappears on the scene, Bill sees a golden opportunity to not only reassert his authority, but to have some much needed fun.

Yet all is not as it appears. For this new enemy is far more powerful than any Billy has ever had to deal with before and he's about to discover that he's finally pushed his luck too far.

But this time it isn't the law that he has to worry about, it's something far more dangerous.

Published by Caffeine Nights Publishing Spring 2014

The Films of Danny Dyer

Danny Dyer is Britain's most popular young film star. Idolised by Harold Pinter and with his films having taken nearly $50 million at the UK box office, Dyer is the most bankable star in British independent films with one in ten of the country's population owning one of his films on DVD. With iconic performances in such cult classics as The Business, The Football Factory, Dead Man Running, Outlaw and now Vendetta, Dyer is one of the most recognisable Englishmen in the world. For the first time, and with its' subject's full co-operation, this book chronicles his film career in depth, combining production background with critical analysis to paint a fascinating picture of the contemporary British film industry and its brightest star. Packed with anecdotes from co-stars and colleagues, as well as contributions from the man himself, The Films of Danny Dyer is the ultimate companion to the work of Britain's grittiest star.

Published by Caffeine Nights Publishing 18th Nov 2013

Harry Tyler – The Face is Back!

When an angry vigilante takes the law into his own hands the Kent police are stumped. But could the brutal serial killer be taking his cues from an outspoken rightwing newspaper columnist? Jailed South London crime lord Johnny Too agrees to be the bait to lure him into the open and end his reign of murder and terror. There's just one problem – he wants retired undercover detective Harry Tyler, the man who put him away, to be part of the plot. And Harry's dead. Isn't he?

Published by Caffeine Nights Publishing 14th October 2013